WORLD FAMOUS LOVE ACTS

WORLD FAMOUS LOVE ACTS

STORIES
BRIAN LEUNG

Winner of the 2002
Mary McCarthy Prize in Short Fiction
Selected by Chris Offutt

Sarabande Books
LOUISVILLE, KENTUCKY

Managing Editor
Sarabande Books, Inc.
2234 Dundee Road, Suite 200
Louisville, KY 40205

Library of Congress Cataloging-in-Publication Data

Leung, Brian.
    World famous love acts : stories / by Brian Leung.— 1st ed.
      p.   cm.
    "Winner of the 2002 Mary McCarthy Prize in Short Fiction, selected by
Chris Offutt."
    ISBN 1-889330-16-7 (pbk. : alk. paper)
    I. Title.
    PS3612.E824 W67 2004
    813'.6—dc21   2003011923

Cover and text design by Charles Casey Martin

Manufactured in Canada
This book is printed on acid-free paper.

Sarabande Books is a nonprofit literary organization.

 This project is supported in part
by an award from
the National Endowment for the Arts.

SECOND PRINTING

For my families, for Taylor, Damien, and Seth,
and, always, for the lost men.

CONTENTS

ACKNOWLEDGMENTS

Grateful acknowledgement is made to the following publications in which versions of these stories were first published:

Story: "Six Ways to Jump Off a Bridge"
Grain: "White Hand"
Salt Hill: "Leases"
Gulf Coast: "Fire Walk: An Old-Fashioned AIDS Story"
The Bellingham Review: "Drawings by Andrew Warhol"
River City: "World Famous Love Acts"

Thank you to Indiana University and *Indiana Review,* Ledig House, University of Cincinnati, the California State University, Northridge College of Humanities Faculty Fellow Program, Catherine Di Tomaso, and Yee-shing Leung. For their friendship, dedication to writing and support of my work, I would also like to thank Adam McComber, Matthew Brim, Nikki Moustaki, Thomas Alvarez, Elizabeth Haymaker, Simeon Berry, Photopresse, Roland Thompson, Scott Russell Sanders, Kirby Gann, Tony Ardizzone, Cornelia Nixon, Alyce Miller, Kate Braverman, Mary Bush, Lois Rosenthal, William Reiss, and Alice Estes Davis.

FOREWORD
Chris Offutt

For five years I held visiting-writer positions at the University of New Mexico, University of Montana, Morehead State University, and The Iowa Writers' Workshop. The combined workload involved nineteen writing classes, each of which lasted a semester, requiring me to read an average of five short stories per week. In addition, I read dozens of thesis manuscripts filled with short stories by graduating students, seventy-five short stories by people seeking admission to a graduate program, and another hundred stories to gauge financial aid. I also taught four seminars that specialized in short fiction.

Recently I took a break from teaching. To make ends meet I judged four fiction contests. Two of them were specific to short stories, and the other two were dominated by collections of short fiction. I may not be an expert on the form, but I certainly know a little something about it.

First of all, writing a good short story is the most difficult task a writer can face aside from producing monthly rent. Secondly, the people who read short stories love them, the majority of said readers being fellow practitioners of the form. Thirdly, a good story will intensify your existence in the short term, and teach you about life in the long run. In other words, it will knock your socks off, blow your hair back, and turn you inside out. A good short story is better than travel, sex, drugs, a symphony, a museum, a massage, watching a sunset, or walking alone in the woods. An entire book of good stories is rare. You are holding just such a book.

To read the well-made short story is a case of briefly entering someone's life by surrendering to the glorious conduit of language. For dramatic reasons, the writer often chooses a person facing a crucial juncture in life. Neither the protagonist nor the situation need to be extraordinary—merely rendered with clarity. The reader becomes privy to the protagonist's innermost thoughts and emotions, expressed through action and yearning— identical to the way you and I reveal intimacies to friends we trust. Part of the writer's job is to generate a similar level of trust from the reader. Brian Leung does precisely that.

He gains trust the old-fashioned way—through confidence, craftsmanship, and compassion. There are no shortcuts here, no tricks or gimmicks, no glib patinas to conceal weak under-pinnings. Brian Leung writes first and foremost about people who react in a genuine fashion to the circumstances around them. The dialogue reads like people talking rather than the product of a writer sitting alone in a room trying to write sentences that will sound like people talking. These are men, women, and children facing personal dilemmas in the contemporary world. They are in a vulnerable state, and it is through their vulnerabilities that we get to know them—just as in real life.

The characters may be nothing like you. Still, they are familiar due to the honesty of their emotional responses to our shared world. By gaining knowledge of their feelings, you will understand the characters—precisely as you get to know people in the actual world.

I have never met Brian Leung, however I now feel as if I possess a modicum of insight into his personality. Not what he looks like or the sound of his voice—the surface traits that distinguish people in a group—but how the writer thinks, where his loyalties lie, his sensitivity to the world. I may be completely mistaken, but it doesn't really matter. The work made me feel as if I was interacting with life lived. True art always does that.

This is a book about loss, twined irrevocably with hope, a hope that surges below the surface of all life, of literary characters on the page, within the private thoughts of every nameless face on the street, in a park, the mall, or a library—the same hope you and I feel at varying times. Ultimately, it is hope that sustains us in life. Hope is stronger than faith, love, belief, loyalty, honor—the list is endless as it is powerful. More than any of the virtues, it is hope that allows us to endure.

Twentieth-century philosophers suggested that humanity must learn to live without hope. What a sad world that would undoubtedly produce; and if one looks at the history of our last century, that sadness is manifest across every continent. The very media that brings us the sadness is in itself quite sad and lacking hope. It has become convention to accept hopelessness and to teach that to the next generation. The stories of Brian Leung contradict such thinking. Read them and see a bold new writer making himself vulnerable on the page.

He gives us all hope.

Six Ways
to Jump Off a Bridge

———||||||||———

Understand Blue Falls, how it got its name, how in dry years, in autumn, water slips over a flat edge, sheer and perfect, a wide liquid sheet reflecting a clear day—blue as an unraveling bolt of satin. But most years are not dry and most days are not completely blue. Not this morning, certainly, as Parker Cheung leans on the railing of the deck behind his home where he sees the falls and the observation bridge bisecting the line of water. Today is misty and the falls are loud, full after three days of rain. And there are people on the bridge. Parker counts four, one of them the sheriff, Katie Buckle. Someone's gone and jumped again, he says to himself. He takes a last drink of tea and walks inside, shaking his head.

Parker considers his dark living room, the *National Geographics* and *Reader's Digests* stacked everywhere, the mugs with their various levels of evaporating green tea. The answering machine in the corner blinks a single unchecked message. It could be his daughter Susan, but he's afraid it won't be and so he's left it alone all morning trying not to think about it. Parker looks outside at the bridge, searching for the sheriff again. She'll be around soon to ask what he knows. At first he doesn't see her, but then she's back on the bridge, a brown-and-khaki thickness with a heavy walk. Maybe I've still got time, he thinks, turning to straighten the room, something he's still not used to even though it's been two years since his wife died. This was her part of their marriage, running the house, raising their daughter. He took care of the egg ranch, *Cheung's Eggs "Something to Crow About!"* But now that his wife is gone, he's shut down the business, and he hasn't spoken to his daughter in nine years. But there is the message on the machine that came while he was showering and it could be Susan. She might have remembered today would have been her mother's sixtieth birthday.

Parker starts by collecting the dirty cups, setting them in the already-full sink. He turns on the tap and hot water sputters out. The kitchen smells like fish, more so than usual, and he remembers last night's meal. He lifts the lid off a cast-iron pot, the head of a small red snapper offering a milky stare, a xylophone of bones strung behind. He throws the fish out the kitchen window and watches for a moment as three cats that he insists are not his fight over the carcass. Beyond them is the bridge from a slightly different angle. Everyone has left except the sheriff. She is facing away, toward the falls, resting both hands on the railing. That's not the side people usually jump from, Parker thinks. It's too close to the falls. The water isn't shallow enough for death and no one jumps off Blue Falls Bridge just to get seriously injured.

The first one to go over was Jason Glass. He was sixteen. Parker saw it, too. It was in the evening, he remembers, after dinner. They had steamed salmon dumplings and bok choy. He was full and walked out on the deck while his wife and daughter cleared the table. The night was cool and it now seems an important detail to him that it rained the next morning and didn't stop for three days. It was dusk and the bridge looked like something etched, a sequence of thick black lines. He saw someone pacing, not some- one, actually, just a form moving back and forth. Finally the figure stopped, and a voice cracked through the twilight air, the form bolting across the bridge. It was running, yelling "I'm Superman!" as it pushed off the rail.

Parker shuts off the water until there is just a small whining stream for rinsing. He starts with the silverware because that's how his wife had always done it. The water is warm and the wetness makes his hands look almost young. He thinks again of the Glass boy. He has never forgotten the sound of Jason's body hitting the rocks, the solitary thump, barely a sound at all. Now, remembering, it is not important to him that he ran inside and startled Annie and Susan, could hardly produce words, nor that somehow he called the sheriff. It is the sound of Jason's body meeting ground, how his life ended as a whisper, in a riverbed, the almost powdery tenor of it as if the world couldn't care if he was a boy or a sack of flour. A reporter for the *Northwest Trader* asked him to describe what it was like to see the young man end his life. Parker watched the reporter's hand scribbling notes on a small pad. How could he describe a person's life dissolving into night air, the shocking lack of reverberation? He was quiet for a moment and the reporter stopped writing, his pencil a fraction of an inch from the paper. Finally, Parker spoke. "It's like reading a sentence and arriving at a comma with nothing after it."

Later, it turned out that Susan knew Jason. She was a year behind him in high school. In the four days before his funeral, she didn't go to class, she stayed home, took meals in her room where she and her mother talked for hours. Once, Parker heard her crying alone. He stopped and knocked on her door but she didn't answer. "I just want you to know," he said, speaking into the wood frame, "there was nothing you could do. They're saying it was drugs. He was causing his parents a lot of trouble." She began crying louder and he put his hand on the doorknob but did not go in. Instead, he waited for his wife to get home.

Now, he has a message on the machine. There's no reason to think it's Susan except that it's his wife's birthday and no one ever calls. And why would she want to talk now after all these years? Parker isn't even sure of what he should say. There are ideas, forms of apology that sift through his mind nearly every day, but they all seem as vague as the reasons he and Susan stopped speaking in the first place.

As Parker washes the dishes, he keeps his eye on the sheriff. He watches her pace slowly as if she's trying to figure something out. But, as far as he's concerned, there's nothing to figure out. They should just tear down the bridge. Aren't six jumpers enough? Building it had seemed like a good idea at the time, but now.... Parker remembers when it first went up, and before that, too, when the Chamber of Commerce held a meeting in the VFW hall, well before Seattle had its Space Needle. There wasn't any reason to come to Washington then, unless you liked lumber, or perhaps cared to see the Columbia covered by a flotilla of logs. He remembers how Joe and Ruth Kent took a summer road trip in their Thunderbird and came back with pictures of gigantic concrete cows, the names of cities painted on their sides, invariably followed by a slogan beginning with "World's Greatest" or "World's Largest." Either that, or it was the home of something or the birthplace of someone. He recalls the Chamber president passing around postcards and salt-and-pepper shakers the Kents bought, all of them bearing the name of a town. There was a picture of a huge ear of corn weighing down a pickup truck. From Las Vegas, they brought back a pair of plastic slot-machine shakers. They said Blue Falls needed an identity, a reason to come and spend money.

Parker feels the edge of a chipped cup and, for a moment, considers throwing it away; about as long, he thinks, as it took to decide on building the bridge. Parker remembers that was a dry year and everyone had fresh in their minds how simple and beautiful the falls were, how glassy and reflective. Everyone thought people would certainly drive to see them. Mildred Thomas was even smart enough to recommend they hire a photographer to take pictures before the bridge went up because that would be better for postcards. By then, Parker had only owned the egg ranch a few years, bought with money he inherited from his father, a purchase he knew he would never have approved of. His father never wanted Parker to do any manual labor.

With the last of the inheritance, Parker put up most of the money for the bridge and he remembers how everyone started calling him by his first name, or tried to. That was when he still wanted people to use his Chinese name, Pak. Only Annie called him Pak, and even she preferred her American name over Ling. He remembers she, too, wanted the bridge, even proposed to the Chamber that they write Pat Boone to see if he would dedicate the bridge when it was done. Her accent was still so thick then he had to translate what she wanted.

We were all a mess, Parker thinks, searching the dishwater for any stray silverware, almost laughing. Pat Boone never wrote back, and Parker's wife stopped playing his records. Worse, though, after all the money invested in postcards and plaques made from diagonally-cut pine limbs, no one could ever say for sure if even one extra person had come into town because of the bridge, though Parker did report he spotted a family on it one summer a couple years after it opened. For about a week the people of Blue Falls allowed themselves to feel vindicated.

Now, forty years later, just as many people know it as Jumper's Bridge. Parker watches the sheriff tap her hand on the railing. It won't be long before she's knocking on his door.

The deeply-stained bottom of one of the cups Parker has already washed gives him an excuse to turn his attention away from the window. He looks at the age spots on back of one of his hands. Old, he thinks, returning his attention to the cup. He considers what he remembers about last night so he'll have it all straight for the sheriff, though he's sure there was nothing out of the ordinary. He wonders who jumped this time, what was the reason. Sometimes, you have connections with these people. Like Jason Glass. It wasn't until years later, months after Susan moved to Los Angeles for college, that Annie turned to him in bed one night, shook her head, and told him the truth. It had come out of nowhere. "Remember Jason Glass?" Her hair was still long and black then, just starting to show a few strands of white.

Parker nodded, a bit startled. He was halfway into a textbook on light therapy and he set it on his lap. "Of course, the one Susan knew."

"She his girlfriend. They fight over his drugs."

He didn't know what to think. "Why didn't one of you say something?" He looked at his wife. "I could have talked to her."

She sat up in bed, her face tightening. "No. You wouldn't. You always too busy with the egg ranch. That your problem. Always your problem."

His wife stayed mad at him for days, which seemed unreasonable to him. Susan had gotten over Jason, hadn't she? After the funeral she started working a few hours a week at the egg ranch as a candler. That first week, he'd asked her as she inspected the back-lit eggs running by on a conveyer belt. "Are you okay?"

Susan did not look up from the eggs. "Fine, Pop."

"Good." Parker walked away. Now he thinks he should have said more. But she did seem fine, busy, occupied at least. And hadn't they later chosen a good career for Susan when she went away to study engineering? She'd even met a nice Chinese boy. At that point, at least, everything seemed okay. What more could they have done for her?

As he dries his hands, there's a knock at the door and he knows it's Katie. Parker goes to open it and catches a glimpse of himself in the dusty hallway mirror. He's still in his terry-cloth robe, the sleeves rolled up for the dishes. The thin rim of his white hair bristles out all over.

He greets Katie with a calm smile.

"There's been another one, Parker."

He nods but does not invite her in. "I saw you over there." He and Katie go back a long way. When she was sixteen, working at the egg ranch was her first job. Parker made her an egg candler, too, but she complained after only a day about the boredom so he moved her to the chicken houses, gave her a boy's job to teach her a lesson. By the end of the summer, she'd become his best worker. It wasn't long before he had her supervising other employees, including Susan. Even though she's in her forties now, thicker, her blonde hair cropped long ago, it is not hard for him to believe this woman with the gun at her side is the same Katie.

"See anything?"

"Not this time," Parker says, looking beyond her to see what she's staring at. The ranch is wet and shiny, the spring weeds in his wife's old hyacinth bed bent from early morning rain. "I really should get out here and do some yard work," he says, but there's no conviction in it. There would never have been flowers at all if not for Annie. He remembers how mad she was one year when she asked him to bring home lavender hyacinth bulbs—not the packaged kind, the bulk—so he could pick out good ones. The next year the whole bed came up white, though he swore he double-checked the bin label. Of course, he hadn't. It never mattered to him.

Katie shakes her head and scuffs a boot into the dark, wet ground. "Your cats are looking a bit scruffy."

"I don't claim them. They claim me."

"Not very smart cats," Katie says, turning around.

"Doesn't seem right the way the place is all closed down."

"A man can't work all his life."

Katie smiles and takes off her plastic covered hat. "You? Work?"

Stifling a smile and crossing his arms, Parker leans against the door frame. "As I remember, I spent most of my time picking up after you."

"Listen you old coot. Gonna invite me in or not?"

Parker finally smiles and gestures her inside. "I suppose you're operating on that permanent warrant you keep telling me about."

She sits on the couch, lays her felt hat on a stack of *National Geographics*. "Jesus. So this is where the old growth forests are ending up."

"Got 'em at Henderson's yard sale. I like to read."

"I remember. But your taste used to run a little more sophisticated. And Jesus. Do you read with night-vision goggles?" She leans over and switches on a lamp.

Parker sits in his recliner, the arms so worn the wood frame shows in places. "Donated my books to the library." He sees the answering machine, the red light blinking over Katie's shoulder. "I can open the curtains."

As he gets up, Katie says, "I've seen enough of the bridge, thank you."

It is dark in here Parker thinks, turning on a reading light. It casts Katie's face in a dim yellow, accentuating the wrinkles around her eyes. He measures her expression. She's not smiling anymore. "Was it bad?"

"It's always bad. But this time the body floated downstream and some kids found it." She pauses and leans forward. "Anything unusual at all last night? No lights? Voices?"

He had gone to bed early, had lain awake a long time thinking about Annie, about the next day being her birthday, and he was a bit ashamed he remembered the occasion now that she was gone. When she was alive, their daughter had to remind him almost every year. He recalls being awake long enough to watch the moonlight shift across the room, long enough to notice the clouds roll in. He'd fallen asleep to the sound of rain. "Nothing," he says, glancing again at the answering machine.

"This guy didn't leave a car or a bike or anything. He went out of his way to get to the bridge. We're just trying to make sure he jumped on his own."

"Maybe he isn't a jumper at all," Parker says. "Just some unlucky guy who fell in."

Katie has already started shaking her head. "I'd like to think that, too, but he's pretty bashed up and we can see where he hit. Head first. Left half his skull behind."

"Local?"

"No I.D. But he was wearing a hunting vest and work boots, so he's from not too far."

"I don't understand how they get so crazy." Ed Cane had gone over something like this, Parker remembers. Got fired from his job as a welder at the Bonneville dam three weeks after his wife and kids moved away to Idaho. He just drove out to the bridge, weighed down his pink slip and divorce papers under a rock, and jumped.

It was summer and hot and everything smelled like burnt pine. Parker had gone out for firecrackers for the Fourth of July picnic. When he came home, Annie rushed out to the truck to tell him. One of the workers saw Ed jump. Said he stood on the rail, shrugged, and dove straight as a pencil.

Katie checks her watch. "You got any coffee, Parker?"

"Just instant." Parker begins to get up but Katie stops him.

"I'll hunt around for it," she says.

He listens as Katie fills the kettle with water, opens the cupboards and drawers, looks for coffee, sugar, and a spoon. He could easily tell her where to look, but he likes the sound of someone else in the kitchen. Annie had always risen a half-hour before him and he sometimes stayed in bed just to listen. Even when Susan was born, he didn't mind the sound of her crying late at night. It was what made the house alive, these sounds coming from upstairs or somewhere down the hall, the comfort of hearing his daughter brushing her hair, the repetitive wisp of it, and the early clack of pans and breakfast dishes, how he could tell just by sound, before he left their room, whether they were having eggs or pancakes, sausage or bacon.

Even in those later years before Susan left for college, when they rarely spoke, Parker could listen to the house and somehow that was enough. How many times had he come inside from work and heard Susan playing too-loud music in her room and said nothing? Now he's beginning to believe that was a mistake, to be the father without a voice. Today, the answering machine blinks silently in front of him while Katie rummages around the kitchen and Parker is still looking for words. If it's Susan, he hopes she's left a number. Twice he's hired people to find her in Los Angeles.

Parker waits until he thinks Katie is done. "Find everything?"

"Just fine," she says from the kitchen. "Maybe they just need a little hope, Parker."

"That's not it. Hope means you know you're missing something." It's more about understanding the lack of something than the possibility, he thinks. After Annie started sleeping in Susan's old bedroom, he believed for a long time she would think better of it and return. But she stayed there, died in that room, too, during her sleep.

Katie sits again, holding her coffee with two hands. "In a way, Parker, I think you're worse off than the rest of us. You've actually seen it happen. The Glass boy before I was sheriff, and the Silva girl."

"That was awful," Parker says. Of all of them, Rebecca Silva's death bothered him and Annie most. She was just twenty-three, the same age as Susan. The jump first looked like an accident, but later, her parents found a note. Her father was a Baptist minister in Tacoma. The newspaper photo pictured her as fair-skinned, with red hair and a wide smile that showed only upper teeth. The story reported she was three months pregnant. Parker saw her sitting on the rail. She was wearing a white sweater and jeans. It was a late afternoon in autumn. The falls were beautiful and though he was concerned at first, he thought she looked relaxed because she was swinging her feet staring at the water. Suddenly, she leaned backward and was gone. "Annie was upset for a long time over that one," Parker says. "She wanted us to move after it happened."

"I remember. She went around trying to get people to tear down the bridge, too."

Parker looks at Katie, surprised. "I didn't know that."

"Oh sure. After the Silva girl, Annie tried to convince anyone who'd listen that we should wrap some explosives around the braces and blow it up."

"She had a point." Parker wonders though, if it was really the bridge she was concerned with. When the Silva girl jumped, Annie was already upset because things were going badly with Susan. She had quit school. There had been a letter, a note really. Parker even recalls the color of the ink, a thick green that soaked into the open spaces in her handwriting. It said *Dear Mom, I'm leaving school. I can't be an engineer. All I've learned is how nothing lasts.* The next day, Rebecca Silva jumped, and Annie was on the phone with Susan, crying, making plans to fly to Los Angeles.

Katie sets down her coffee and walks to the long curtains covering the sliding glass doors. She pulls the cord and they shimmy open, gray light wedging in with each pull. She steps outside onto the deck. Mist has settled among the tops of the pines. It makes Parker think of altitude, as if they are much higher than they are, as if his house is on some elevated precipice.

Parker walks outside, tying his robe tightly around his waist as Katie lights a cigarette. The falls are percussive and the sun, a disk beyond the clouds, silvers the bridge. "Sometimes it can be beautiful."

"That's the bitch of it. It's not the bridge." Katie crushes out her barely smoked cigarette. "It's just where they decide to stop being alone. That jump begins a long time before they make it out here."

"I can't figure why they don't snap out of it when they look down at the rocks." As Parker says this, he remembers that Jason Glass had gone over in the night and Sarah went backward. They didn't see where they were falling. What does that feel like, he wonders, the few seconds of going somewhere else before meeting the ground? And what if there is even one synapse of regret, a spark of mistake?

"You need anything else?" Parker says, the urge to check the message growing stronger.

"Guess not," Katie says. "I actually thought we could do it over the phone this time, but you didn't pick up."

"You called?"

"This morning. I left a message." Katie points inside. "See, it's blinking."

Parker hesitates. "I know," he says finally. "I thought it might be Susan. I was waiting until you left."

"Oh, I'm sorry, Parker. You two still haven't spoken?"

"She doesn't want to talk to me," Parker says. He catches the sharpness in his voice and takes a slow breath.

"Jesus. You can't let that crap go on forever."

"I don't even know where she is. The last time I spoke to her she told me not to call."

"All I know is that I've got Jacob off to college and Jamie still at home, and I couldn't live without either of them." Katie smiles and pokes Parker in the side. "Their father's a different story."

Parker does not smile back. He wants to tell Katie how the silence is his fault, how when Susan dropped out of school he would not speak to her. Annie wanted the two of them to go to Los Angeles together to bring Susan back, or at least make sure she was okay, but he refused to indulge her throwing her life away, refused to leave the egg ranch unattended. And he never spoke to Susan; kept a vague tab on her through his wife, but didn't even know her phone number. When Annie returned from L.A., she moved into the other bedroom where she'd stayed for all those years. And when she died, he couldn't reach Susan, couldn't find her listed under the name of Cheung, not under any of the Cheungs he called. There had been the funeral, the white roses over the mahogany casket, everyone from town. He had hoped that somehow Susan would have found out, that his wife had made some plan. But no, there was that whole quiet service without her in the little wooden church he helped paint every five or six years. "That's why I don't sell the place," he tells Katie. "That's why I bought an answering machine."

But Katie is quiet for a few moments. "I'm just small potatoes, but I could call L.A. again for you."

"I don't think so. You already did what you could." Parker's voice is suddenly soft and resigned. "It's my mess."

Katie offers an understanding nod. "So, what am I going to do about all *this* mess? It's only every few years, but they may as well've jumped in the same week." The two of them stand silently for a moment. "Well," Katie says, pulling up on her belt, "I should get going. If you think of anything, I know you have the number."

Parker walks her through the house. He stands on the front steps as she opens her car door. "Maybe this was the last one," he says.

"I'd like to think so," Katie says. "But there's more than six ways to jump off a bridge."

Parker listens to the snap of wet gravel as she pulls away. Then it is quiet except for a few sparrows quarreling in the trees. He looks at the three large chicken houses, still and long as docked ships. The old delivery truck with faded lettering and flat tires sits near the fence, two seasons of unpruned blackberry vines already overtaking the front bumper. It is all so different now, so hushed, no gurgle of chickens working through the tin buildings, no one walking around with cardboard flats or running one of the egg collectors, no one at all. Parker stopped that just after Annie died, laid off people he'd known longer than his own daughter.

He sits in his recliner and focuses on the answering machine's small red light. He watches until it begins to move in tiny circles. This is what it comes to, he thinks. It's not at all how he imagined this stage of his life when he first came to the United States with Annie and they started the business.

Parker takes a quieting breath and swivels around to face the open glass doors and looks out at the bridge. He closes his eyes but it is still there, only in his mind it is even clearer and the sound of Blue Falls becomes the sound of rain, becomes something even softer, the sound of a body dropping through the air. It is like some improvisation of wind. And there is Susan's face, tenuous as a thread of silk beaded with water, glistening, drops falling and again the sound of rain, something more, pushing off, letting go. Parker thinks that this is the sound of decision, what it's like to hear someone jump when not a word is spoken. It is not an act of abandonment. That happened long ago and it was mutual, and no one listened anyway. No one notices unless we've made it all the way down, he thinks. No one hears until we are completely quiet.

Now Annie is gone and unless Susan calls, she's gone too. All that ignored intuition, Parker thinks, those families of the people who jumped missed it completely, all that pointing to the spot on the rail where they jumped. They got it all wrong because it happened well before that. When it comes to the final moment, it's already too late. It started for Ed Cane when his family moved to Idaho, Parker thinks, and when Jason Glass didn't get relief from twenty bucks worth of plastic bag slapped in his palm. It started when Rebecca understood a fetus would be a punishment for the rest of her life. These are the irrevocable moments when we can't see we're already in midair, when we push our daughter so far away she is lost to us, and then our wife goes too and we are alone. Parker imagines a blue descent, mistakes peeling off his shoulders, and finally, in one simple trajectory, the lightness he'd sought after all that awkward navigation, the relief that surprises even him. I've wondered all along, he thinks, and suddenly I know that this is what it feels like when you're falling.

Executing Dexter

———||||||||———

It was a contest to see which of us could inflict the most horrible death on our babies. Grant and I stood on the soppy shore of Lindo Lake, mud hens gurgling in the cattails, their little white beaks and black heads, those beady, undertaker eyes all busying about, more purposeful than the other fowl, I always thought, the blue-green headed mallards and the white farm ducks dumped off each year a few months after Easter, the abandoned and hissing barnyard geese. These would be our accomplices in our last grand effort. The baby was dressed and ready on our raft of plywood and plastic milk bottles, *sleeping*, we said of all the victims during preparations.

I met Grant in Ms. Felder's fourth-grade class earlier that year.

I was a transfer student, unhappily arriving in a school where I was one of three black students. And worse, my father, a hard-nosed, back-to-basics teacher, had joined the faculty. By the second week, the playground was referring to him as Darth Vader. I was such a pariah that even the two other black kids wouldn't speak to me. "Git," they said the first time I talked to them. But Grant didn't hesitate because he could afford to be friends with a kid like me whose parents made him wear Catholic-school uniforms in a public school, navy blue Toughskins and white button-up shirts that didn't tuck in over my fat little belly. Grant was the kind who wanted everyone to like him and everyone did, though before me, he said he didn't hang out with anyone. He'd gotten his father's dark eyes and Native-American hair that he feathered back on both sides, and much of his mother's dewy skin. In school photos, he stood in the rear because he was five inches taller than the next tallest kid. But it's not his height that stands out in those photographs, it's his already perfect smile, those straight white teeth that got him into R movies and allowed him to turn in homework late.

"You ready for this?" I asked him as I strapped our baby to the raft. We'd both spent our allowances buying loaves of bread to make the body. This one was a boy and we called him Dexter—a small burlap sack full of bread with strategically placed beak-sized holes. For limbs we used tube socks, for the head, a half-deflated supermarket ball, the ninety-nine cent kind in the tall cages, the ones we bugged our moms to buy us but which never lasted more than a few days. For Dexter's face, we drew large eyes and a small blue frown.

"I'm not sure this is going to work," Grant said. He ran a hand through his perfectly parted hair, stopping in the middle. "Has he been a bad baby?"

"Guess so," I offered. It was the first time he'd asked that question. "Aren't they all bad babies?" I finished the last of my knots.

Grant took his hand from his head, his shiny hair floating back to its original position, as if commanded. He bent down next to me. "We'll have to think about what he's done."

The first baby to go was Veronica—Grant's idea, a five-pound sack of flour with a red felt-tip smile and two googly eyes plucked out of a stuffed giraffe's head we found in the Goodwill donation box. We made her in Grant's room, the only place where we had any privacy. My house was out. Even though, in those days, my mother was just an echo in my life, always doing something besides being home, and my father expected me to read, or practice for a recital. There was always a recital. I stayed out until nearly five o'clock when I knew my father came home from school. I was supposed to spend that time doing something constructive, but I knew I'd be locked down once he got home and there'd be plenty of time, too much time, in our quiet house.

But Grant lived in the Pink Ghetto, a low-rent apartment complex coated with stucco the color of chewed bubble gum. His room was safe to build babies. His stepfather—Grant called him "Dude"—had two jobs, one as a bouncer at a local cowboy bar, the other selling gas, so he was rarely home. And Grant's mother never bothered us because she had to lie flat during the last three months of her pregnancy. At first, I never saw her face, just her creamy white feet beyond the half-opened door. "Hello, Herschel," the feet said the day we finished Veronica. "You boys behaving?"

I looked directly at those feet as one scratched the other with its big, saucer-shaped toenails. "Yes, Mrs. Pope."

Veronica lay peacefully on Grant's floor waiting to be dressed. "I wish she'd hurry up and have that stupid baby," Grant said as he slipped one of his old T-shirts over Veronica's square body. "I hate being quiet all the time. I don't know why Dude let her get pregnant anyway."

I sat Veronica up and held her for Grant's inspection. He frowned, handing me some markers. "You can't hurry a baby," I said. "They got to eat 'n stuff before they come out." I plumped her red, kewpie mouth and filled in doelike lashes over Veronica's loopy eyes, her black plastic pupils swirling with each jostle.

"What do you think they eat while they're inside?"

I paused. When Grant wasn't the expert, I took the opportunity to show him I knew something. "Milk," I said, looking around his room. The best thing about being at Grant's was his posters, every wall a pipeline wave with a surfer crouched and peering out. My favorite was the blonde guy with the green eyes that Grant said got killed in Hawaii surfing storm waves. But Grant liked the one of Farah, head tilted back, a mane of frosty blonde hair scattered around her face, nipples perked beneath a red one-piece.

"She's a fox," he said for the hundredth time, noticing I was looking at her. "Milk comes from the boobs," he said, trying to correct me.

"Oh, women got these tubes inside that the baby sucks on like a straw." I held up Veronica again and Grant was satisfied.

We discussed how unborn babies ate as we walked to the bridge that stretched across the dry bed of the San Diego River. Following my tube principle, by the time we arrived in the center, we agreed that babies had access to certain foods right after the mother swallowed them. The thought of a baby sucking down chewed spaghetti grossed us out to the point of laughter.

Grant held Veronica over the concrete railing. The air was warm and breezy. Forty feet below us was the sandy riverbed, clotted here and there with bamboo stands. Veronica's indifferent pucker mocked us now and I didn't feel sorry for her at all as Grant let go and she turned head first, the T-shirt flailing like a comet tail. She thudded into a big white spray of flour, carnationlike. Not as gruesome as we hoped, but still worth the effort. Little white puffs blew off her like smoke. "That's so trick," Grant said. "She's dead and on fire." He looked at me, the bright sun glaring off his black hair. "Your turn, Hersch."

Just then a sheriff's car stopped next to us. "What are you boys up to?" the man in the car said. He was asking both of us but looking at me. This was the kind of person I had to watch out for, the kind my father explained about the day we moved into this town. "You might meet ignorant people here who are uncomfortable with blacks," he said. He never used words like "racist" or even "prejudiced." There were a few kids on the playground who fit my father's definition and let me know, called me Fat Albert or Cosby Kid, but Grant was always there, so I felt ahead of the game.

The sheriff waited for our answer about what we were doing. "Nothing," we offered at the same time.

"You from around here, son?" the sheriff asked me. "Don't recognize you."

"Yes, sir," I said. I hadn't ever talked to the police by myself. "I live over on Julian." I looked at the ground and then back up. I turned to Grant who just smiled, and I felt safe.

The sheriff pouched his tongue behind his bottom lip and shook his head. "Oh, you're part of that teacher's family. Okay then. You boys better move along. Don't be hanging around on this bridge. Someone's like to come by and throw you off."

Grant and I ran, relieved, laughing all the way back to his apartment. It was all we could do to be quiet when we got there. The feet were sleeping. I'd seen them enough to know, kind of curved in toward each other. Grant went in his mother's bedroom but I stayed in the hallway. He brought out an empty pitcher and went to the kitchen, filling it with water and ice. "That was so smooth," Grant whispered. "We were so smooth." One thing I always liked about Grant is that he talked like TV people, at least the ones I snuck watching when my parents were asleep or outside. Grant took the ice water into his mother's room and we met on his bed. We lay side-by-side, feet to heads.

"I'll come up with something good for next time," I said, staring at the green-eyed surfer.

"Better be," Grant answered in an unexpected squeak. And then he said it again so it came out right. "Better be."

Grant wasn't as excited about floating Dexter as he had been. We already had two under our belt, Veronica, and James, who we hung, twice. Dexter, we planned to shove into the middle of the lake where hungry ducks and geese would then flock, devouring his insides, leaving behind his pink, plastic head and burlap skin. Grant and I sat at the edge of the lake, staring at our bread-plumped creation with his sad blue smile. On the opposite shore, a late morning bullfrog started its deep call, that drawn out plea that sometimes sounded to us like a grown man's voice calling for his mother—*M o m . . . M o m . . . M o m . . . M o m*—and sometimes—*b o n e . . . b o n e . . . b o n e . . . b o n e*.

"We should wait," Grant said. He'd been moody all morning.

I felt the wet earth soaking through to my butt so I sat up on my heels. "Wait for what? It's all done. We just have to push him in the water."

"There ain't enough ducks yet, anyway."

"The minute we throw a piece of bread out there there'll be millions."

Grant offered a soft laugh. "Greedy little fuckers." He stood up and tapped his sneaker against one of the four milk bottles that would keep the raft afloat. "I kissed Delia Sanchez. I forgot to tell you."

This was big news and just like Grant to say something out of the blue like that. Most of the other kids made fun of her, but Grant thought Delia was the prettiest girl in our class, even with her prosthetic arm with its steel claspers. She wore the best clothes, usually yellow, which showed off her brown skin, darker even than mine. One time she wore a green hoop skirt to school for show-

and-tell but she kept it on all day. On the playground, she dared Grant and me to climb underneath. "Is she a good kisser?" I asked.

"Real good." Grant smiled, the first genuine one of the morning. "It was so trick, I walked her home yesterday and we went in her bedroom. She has all these pictures of Mexican singers and stuff. But she just turned around and kissed me right on the lips."

"What about her arm? Did it poke you or anything?"

Grant gave me one of his "You're an idiot" looks. "Anyway, her mom came home right then."

I was secretly glad that Delia's mother interrupted them. I knew Grant liked Delia, but I didn't appreciate the idea of my only friend being taken away. I felt like he was pretty much all I had. And at that age, Grant was already having feelings for girls I could only pretend at. When I suggested the name Veronica for our first baby, it was as close as I could get to Delia, I thought, without being obvious.

Grant kneeled next to Dexter, checking the twine I'd used to bind him. "Anyways, Dude found out. Delia told her dad and he came over. Dude was screaming at me all night. Mom even got out of bed to make him calm down." Grant ran a hand through his hair and shook it out.

"He's a jerk," I said, which I always knew was what Grant wanted to hear about his stepfather.

"A prick." Grant stood, looking straight down at Dexter. His expression hardened. "Pack some more bread in his arms and let's do this," he said.

———

Hanging James from the rafters in our horse corral was my idea. I was smart about it. The day before, I asked my father in my most polite voice if Grant could play at our house. My father looked up from the papers he was grading. His small brown eyes were bloodshot. If my mother had been there, she would have reminded him to put on his reading glasses. "We want to build a fort in the backyard," I told him.

My father hmmphed and looked at the fat gold harp in the living room, scratching his temple with his red grading pen. "What about practice?" He sat straight back in his chair so I had to look up at him. He reminded me that my grandmother got the harp from a woman whose house she cleaned for thirty-two years. I focused, as always, on the ridge of pebbly moles which formed dark brown cornices over his cheeks. "You know, Herschel," he said, "success is all about execution. You can't have good execution without practice."

I nodded like I always did when he was speaking. My father had a way of making me feel that I didn't have a clue as to what was valuable in life. Even years later, when I was long out of the house and just visiting, he'd find some way of bringing up the dusty harp I couldn't play and the wife I never had. Though I knew he loved me, when I was young, I often felt my father didn't see me so much as a boy, but as a kind of dullard robot he was trying to reprogram. That day, when I'd been thoroughly lectured on how life was a series of wisely and expertly executed acts, we agreed I'd practice the harp twice as long that afternoon and Grant could come play.

All that string plucking was worth having Grant over the next day. It was the first time I'd been allowed to have a friend visit and somehow Grant made my backyard much more interesting. We lived on two acres of eucalyptus trees and granite rock. The people before us owned a horse and for some reason, even though he'd never ridden, my father thought we'd own one, too. The corral sat in the very corner of our property, a dusty, gnawed-wood square with a plywood shed in one corner.

Grant hung by his arms from one of the rafters as I prepared all the things to make our victim—two pimento olives for eyes and miniature marshmallows for the mouth. Grant's corduroys belled slightly over his tennis shoes at my eye-level, one of them with a hole big enough that I could see his dirty white sock. "Got the pantyhose?" I asked. He dropped to the ground and pulled from his pocket a pair of his mother's nylons and an unbelievably long length of twine.

We began filling James' nylon body with dirt, tying it off in places so it would hold. "What if this were a real baby?" Grant said, scooping dirt into what would become the torso.

"We wouldn't do it if it were a real baby," I said.

"No, I mean real like a person." Grant stopped scooping dirt and crossed his legs. He tapped the ends of his fingers together, his nails already black. "Like, what if my mom's baby isn't just a baby, it's already a kid?"

I kept building James, but I was trying to get what Grant meant. "You don't just come out a person," I said.

Grant climbed back up to the rafter, hanging himself from his already-long arms, the ones that would end up years later being good for basketball and baseball and the pole vault. "So when does it happen? When does a baby turn into a real person?"

"I think they gotta talk."

"Like, 'Dadda?'"

"No. Sentences. 'I want juice.' Like that."

Grant swung a bit, the tips of his shoes waving in front of me as I started packing James' head. I could tell he was forming a question. "But what if it's a stupid baby?"

I was getting frustrated because Grant wasn't helping. I stood and looked at him. "Then it's not a real person, I guess."

Grant let himself down from the rafter one more time. "How do we even know if *we're* people yet?" he said. Pausing in exasperation, he added, "Surfers don't have babies." Just then, a small whirlwind kicked up and ran through the corral, and Grant leapt into the middle of it, the twisting air pulling his black hair all about his face. He stretched his arms out, laughing, following the whirlwind out the corral gate and into the yard until it plunged through the fence and into the neighbor's property. That night I'd dream that I jumped into the whirlwind, too, and that it lifted us both up and floated us away.

"That was so trick," Grant said, returning to the shed. We sat down next to James, and Grant started making his version of a noose out of the twine while I began toothpicking James' face until he had two pimentoed eyes and a broad, white, marshmallow mouth. But the oddest part about James was the large nylon rosette formed by tying off the waistband at the top of his head. This baby, we decided, was deformed.

"He smiles like you," I said.

Grant stood up and tossed the noose over the rafter. "I saw Dude with some lady," he said in yet another of his surprise revelations. "My mom sent me to get some money from him at the gas station and this chick was sitting in the garage with him, rubbing his shoulders."

"Maybe they were just friends," I said, though I could tell by Grant's look that I wasn't convincing. "Okay," I said. "That stinks." I lifted James up so Grant could slide the noose around his neck.

"She had all these rings on her fingers and a butterfly tattoo on her shoulder. I just stared at him and told him *Mom* sent me to get some money for the store. And that chick didn't even flinch. She just smiled and called me a cutie or something like that and kept her hands on Dude's shoulders." Grant pulled on the twine, leaving a bit of slack when I lifted James above my head for the hanging. "You're so lucky you got a good dad," he said.

That almost made me drop James right then. I'd never heard anyone say that. But somehow I understood why he would. My dad gave me hardly any freedom and Grant had all he wanted, and it didn't make him any happier. But I was also surprised because I'd often secretly had the thought that I would have liked Grant's stepfather as *my* dad, someone who would dip my head in the toilet for pretend punishment and let me out of the truck to pee just about anytime I had to go. Someone, I realized, who had no parenting skills at all but did what he could. I thought about Grant's proposition. "I guess," I finally said. And then, as James began to get heavy on my upstretched arms, "Ready?"

I let go of James and our makeshift noose tightened, his head flopping slightly to the side, one eye popping off. But in seconds, the sand began to ooze through the noose, James' baby-head diminishing, his marshmallow mouth plunking off as the nylon fabric shifted through the rope, the other eye, with its dead pimento pupil, falling to the ground just before the now-headless torso flopped on top of it.

Grant laughed as hard as I've ever heard him. All I could think of was my father, that he was right somehow. We hadn't been thoughtful enough. Our execution was poor. "That doesn't count," I said. "It's like if the rope broke. We got to do it again."

I figured out that we'd let too much slack at the top of his head where we tied it off. So I worked out the knot and tied it lower, giving James a broader head, something like a round of cheese. I quickly poked-in a face with the dirty marshmallows and olives. The design was hardly symmetrical but it would do.

"Poor dude looks confused," Grant said.

We went through the process again, and that time James hung, face intact. He spun slowly in front of us, his dazed eyes coming around to meet ours, the brownish-white mouth looking suddenly like a frown. There was hardly a sound, the solitary clack of eucalyptus bark falling to the ground, a dog barking blocks away. Grant and I stared at James while his gentle revolutions slowed. I think both of us were surprised at how possible what we'd done was.

The morning breeze blew just as we knew it would. We were ready to shove Dexter, our white-bread infant, into the lake. He'd been our most perfectly executed plan up to that point—body and flotation design, material acquisition, shore location, Teacher Prep Day when all the kids were off, the time, it was all thorough. Grant sprinkled the remainder of the bread around the small raft, placing the bulk of it so the ducks would find the openings we'd cut in the burlap body. The last step was tying twine to the back of the raft in order to retrieve the remains.

"That's it," Grant said, pushing the raft into the water. It slowed to a near halt about five feet from shore. From there we planned for the breeze to carry it farther. We sat back and watched, the unraveled twine between us. A redwing blackbird trilled from atop a cattail. Our pink-headed Dexter floated surely, calmly, on the rippled water with not a duck in sight on this side of the lake.

Grant took in a deep breath and let it out slowly. "Do you think there's such things as hexes?" he asked.

"Like voodoo? Sure, maybe." I looked at Grant but he was staring out at the water. A dandelion tuft landed on his head, twirled for moment on point, like a dancer, and floated off. I turned back to Dexter. He was exactly the size of a baby, I thought. The raft was making slow but noticeable progress. "Shoulda made a sail too," I offered.

"Do you think you could put a hex on someone without knowing it?" Grant had sounded serious all morning, and I could tell by the gravity of his voice that these also were not lightly asked questions. "Like if you wanted something to happen but you didn't know you wanted it to happen. But then it did."

"Voodoo curses and stuff can't work unless you believe they can."

"I guess," Grant said.

It took about twenty minutes for Dexter to float out thirty or so yards. Finally, a pair of curious mud hens swam out to the raft and started nibbling at the bread crumbs, their hornlike calls sounding like defective party favors. "Won't be long now," I said. Anytime feeding began, ducks from all over the lake quickly congregated.

"My mom's not pregnant anymore," Grant said softly.

I turned to him but said nothing. He kept his eyes on the lake.

"Dude and I were watching *Hawaii Five-0* and Mom yelled from the bedroom. And Dude didn't want to move her so the ambulance came." Grant stood up and scratched a piece of dried mud off one shoe with the other. He brushed off the back of his pants, the whole time looking out on the lake. Dozens of ducks from all sides were headed toward Dexter, the symmetry of their wakes like one imagines D-day flotillas. A few of the more distant ones took flight.

"What was wrong?" I asked.

"Dude wouldn't let me in the bedroom and I didn't see her till they rolled her out. She had this air thing over her face. I stayed at the neighbors' last night. She's okay. Dude called."

"But she didn't have it?"

"Dude talked to the neighbors and they didn't tell me a whole lot. I get to see her tonight. They just said she lost the baby."

The mud hens and a couple early ducks had finished nibbling away the extra crumbs and had begun taking tentative stabs at the holes in Dexter's burlap body. "I guess a brother woulda been cool," Grant said.

"Yeah," I said, and I meant it, though I knew for me that possibility was out. One time, after a round of questions on the subject, my wearied mother told me while we were buying a baby shower gift that she loved me but that in general she wasn't fond of children and one was all she could handle.

Grant picked up what remained of our twine, the only thing now that connected us to Dexter, the plattered baby we'd sent out to get pecked and probed. I stood up next to Grant, the chill of partially-wet pant legs licking the back of my legs. The bulk of the ducks and a few bulbous geese were feet away from the raft and when they arrived they tore into Dexter from all sides. They were callous in the way that animals are, poking through the burlap where the ribs might be, hollowing out the kneecaps, tearing at the chest. All of it a frenzy. There may as well have been blood spurting about because Grant and I looked at each other at the same time and without saying a word we started yelling at the ducks and he pulled the twine to get Dexter to shore. But the milk bottles that kept him afloat so well were also like left-on emergency breaks and he came back slowly. The ducks and geese and mud hens followed, flapping loudly over one another to get at Dexter's flesh.

Grant pulled the raft in as fast as he could, each tug whooshing it toward us in an almost predictable rhythm. I kept yelling and throwing what few sticks I could find. And when that didn't work, I joined Grant on the twine. To us, at that moment, Dexter was real and human and we had to rescue him. And he wasn't real because there was anything lifelike about him, nor because later we would bury him and have a funeral in my backyard. He was real because we were boys and because we said so, and because with each pull of the line connecting us to him we felt like we were saving ourselves.

Good Company

————|||||||————

W hen those African hands appeared in front of me about a week ago, you might think I would've been scared. But I wasn't, not for a second. I woke up that morning and there they were above my bed kind of prayerlike and attached to nothing but air. They were sugary brown and waxy like they'd worked hard for a lot of years. And when they opened, the palms were pinkish tan and dark brown in all the creases. I reached up to touch them but it was like there was nothing to touch, so I left my hand there for a second to compare. Mine are ivory-gray, and practically the only thing that was the same were our white, beveled fingernails. So far they haven't done much except follow me around but I know they'll do *something*. I have this meeting here at my diner and people expect me to talk and I don't have any idea what I can do to convince them. Maybe they'll be the most important words I'll ever speak, so I figure those hands will pitch in somehow. But like I say, they haven't done anything for a week but float. Right now it feels pretty much like I'm alone in all this. Then again, I've gotten kind of used to that over the years. Not that I wouldn't prefer someone at my side now and then.

I can't be worrying about having some company or what those hands are going to do, especially when this whole place is about to be packed with people wanting free biscuits. It isn't as easy as it used to be either. I make them from scratch and that means the mixing and kneading and rolling out. And these knotty old hands of mine have just about given out for that kind of work. Which is why I'm nearly covered in flour. But this morning's meeting is very important. I can't recall a time when Blue Falls was in more of a fix than right now. All my boys who eat here are mostly loggers or truckers or some such and Washington state just isn't making those jobs the way they used to. And the rest of us make our living serving them, so it's like what they say about falling dominos. And now we have Straymark & Sons who want to come in and buy up the whole street above the river and put in a fancy new hotel. Just wipe out Blue Falls all together.

So that's what I figure those hands came around for. They've been following me since the moment I got out of bed a week ago and they haven't stopped. Even this morning when I was showering. But they never steamed up or got wet. Just sat over my shoulder, and I can barely reach around to wash my own back anymore and maybe could have used some help but I didn't say anything. Then like every morning for the last week, they followed me to work all the way down Sturgeon Road even though sometimes it was hard to tell. There isn't much light at three A.M. except maybe the moon. But they were there the whole time, moving and praying. I started to think it was an angel, but if God sent me one of those, why didn't he send me something that talked? Though I suppose a pair of floating hands is a lot easier to take than a floating pair of lips.

Coming to work so early every morning has been a blessing whether I have a pair of hands praying over me or not. This little town means everything to me and walking through it while everything's so quiet is a special thing. Though I don't have children, I imagine it's like watching your own baby sleeping. It isn't such a sad little place at night because you can't tell the difference between what's closed till morning and what's closed for good. Night time kind of makes it all the same and you can imagine in the morning every store is going to open. It's a sad thing half won't. The last time anything new opened up was a pottery shop. But that guy was crazy. Gil, and he took off after not too long. I think people gave up too early and now they see the boarded-up windows and they want to give up some more. But what they don't get is that they're giving up on each other. This morning is my last chance to help them understand.

It's easy to figure out that these floating hands have come to help me convince everyone not to give up the town. Lord knows the hands haven't done anything else. Though I'm not one to look a gift horse in the mouth. They were an answer to my prayers just like Momma promised me when I was a little girl. She was as

Missouri Irish as you get, but when I was ten and Desdemona turned eight, she sat us down and told about how she thought Jesus might have been black. "I just want you girls to know the world takes some figuring out and I got one thing figured. Those people that lived where Jesus did all got dark skin. It goes that he must've been dark-skinned too." Desdemona and I didn't know what to think until Momma smiled and told us it was a good thing she was telling us.

She took a folded-up map out of her pocket that she probably got from the library where she volunteered twice a month. She spread the map on the kitchen table. The whole world lay flat right there in front of us and Momma pointed out Jerusalem and traced her cracked finger with its dirty nail down to Egypt and kept going through some words that said *Darkest Africa* until she got to the Atlantic. "This side's where they caught slaves," she said. I looked at Desdemona and then up at Momma with that long strand of red hair that always got loose over her right eye. She was smiling but kind of unsure, like a baby taking its first step. "I'm telling you girls this because there's some hateful things going on and I don't want you to take part." We didn't know what she meant. This was before Daddy moved us all up to Washington, so we didn't have TV and our electricity up there in the hills worked only half the time. Any radio we heard was a lucky thing. But Momma went to town nearly every other day and she talked with the other ladies and got news about what was going on down there in Alabama and Mississippi. I guess that's what set her off, though neither Desdemona or I ever asked.

Momma's dried up little finger rested on Africa all carved up in yellows, greens, and oranges. "This is the mother country," she said. "This is where we all come from." After she said this, Momma ran her finger to every spot where white people like us lived and showed us how it was likely everyone started out in Africa and migrated up to the other countries, getting whiter as they went along. I imagined people's skin actually changing color as they traveled across the land. For a few weeks after we had that talk, Desdemona and I watched each other's skin as we walked up to the schoolhouse. But we always stayed pale little redheads. We figured it was only a couple miles, so that's why our skin wouldn't change. Momma's point, with the three of us stooped over that map, was that we were all from the same place. "No matter what you hear," she told us, "don't you never talk down to colored folks. You never know if you might be talking down your own blood." Then Momma said the thing that's always stuck with me. She took down our family Bible, which I always liked because it was covered in blue velveteen, and she set it right next to Africa. "You girls will have trouble in your life and when you do, pray to God and Africa."

That's a lot to think about for a ten-year-old girl but it sure makes a lot of sense now, seeing how I've been visited by these hands that won't even let me go to the bathroom alone, and that's one area where I don't need God to send me any assistance. I suppose it doesn't amount to much if they help something good happen. At least maybe point me in the direction of what I can say to everyone that will change their minds. I even thought that maybe they were going to make these biscuits I'm rolling out even better than usual or maybe I'd just have to fix up one batch.

Then the hands would pray over those and they'd divide up to as many as I needed. I came to my senses, and I'm sure my old Sunday-school teachers would be surprised I actually listened to their stories about miracles.

But I was talking about Momma. There's a lot about a person that just isn't anyone else's business and I don't plan to make a secret about the fact that I have that trouble Momma talked about all those years ago. When she was dying, I took care of her. Doctors said her insides were eaten up with cancer. On the outside, Momma got tireder and tireder until one day she gave out and lay down and went to sleep. I stayed next to her bed all afternoon singing songs and stroking her thin hair. My hands hadn't quite swollen up then and I kept my nails a bit longer. Her hair was white as can be and soft as running your fingers through flour. And that's what I did. I kept running my fingers through it. Sometime late she opened her eyes and said to me very softly, "Madeleine, I'm going home." The nurse was there too and she told me not to worry, Momma was delirious. But I knew she wasn't and I knew what she meant by home. "Sing me my song," she said, and then she closed her eyes and I sang "In the Garden." And I couldn't help but cry when I got to the part that says "he bids me go thro' the voice of woe, his voice to me is calling." And that's what I remember, Momma suddenly breathing soft and my hand running through her thin hair as I stopped singing and everything was absolutely quiet.

I'm as old as Momma was when she went and I haven't been to a doctor, but one of these days not too far off I guess I'm going to go home and lay down and just go to sleep like she did. Only,

I won't have anyone stroking my hair when I go. Certainly not Desdemona. She went off to all sorts of countries where she digs up bones and pottery and hasn't been home since even before Momma died, and if you asked me a couple days ago I would have said I just as soon she never came home.

But that isn't my trouble. That isn't why my prayers brought those African hands. It's all about Blue Falls losing itself to these developers. They like to say "redevelopment" but in my mind it isn't that way if you come in and tear out every little building and put up your own. My diner is one of the places they want. It isn't much, but practically everyone in town comes in at least once a week for breakfast. It's the biscuits they like, and they're always asking for my recipe. All I know is I can charge next to nothing for the eggs and bacon and ask an arm and a leg for the biscuits and they still have to have those. I took this place over from Jacob Velk nearly twenty years ago. He was the happiest old man I ever met and I found out why but I'm too polite to say how many half-empty whisky bottles I came across stuck here and there. I have a real good business and I plan to leave it to my little friend Patrick. I stay quiet about it, but he must be in his thirties. He came back to Blue Falls and started working here, kind of landed in my lap after he broke up. He says "partner" like that hides what he means but I don't think it would matter much around here. Still, we don't bring it up. The funny thing is when he was a boy he stole money right out of the charity box I still keep next to the register—and one day I'll be giving him the place. I'm giving it, that is, if everyone doesn't sell out.

Maybe I'm soft, but this town means just about everything to me. When Daddy moved us here he somehow fixed us up in a pretty nice house. Nicer than the one we had in Missouri anyhow. When we first rode up the house looked so tall and white and the apple orchard was full of small green apples. That was how he planned to make a living, growing apples. Of course, it never worked out that way. Daddy went to work at the dam and it wasn't too many years before he died and the orchard never really produced enough for us to do much with. But Momma worked here and there and somehow we got by. Then Desdemona got the scholarship to go off to college and it was just me and Momma and Blue Falls.

I'm not dumb enough to think that everything will ever be as good as it was when I was a little girl, but it can be better than it is and that doesn't include this company with plans for a big hotel and strip mall Straymark & Sons wants to call *Blue Falls Riverside*. They passed out plenty of attractive color drawings, too. Passed those out as if they were Santa Claus. The pictures showed the hotel with its big blue windows and log siding and the next-door mall, everything bright and clean and the Columbia shimmering on the other side. All anyone could think of was how many jobs they were promising. Before those hands came, floating above me like an angel that was too good to see all of, I figured it was going to happen whether I wanted it to or not. So many of the businesses have shut down anyway. Everyone is saying those buildings are just property waiting to be sold. But even though I may not be around much longer, I'd like to leave a Blue Falls worth living in. I have to find the right words for this meeting and if those hands are going to do something there isn't much time left.

I thought the hands helped when they first came because I got the idea for these free biscuits. I was praying before I went to sleep, praying like I have all these years, just as Momma told me, and this time when I woke up there was Africa ready to help. So after I got over the surprise of it, I sat up and said another prayer and those hands closed up in front of me like they were praying too. I sat for quite a while trying to figure out what to do and those hands kept praying right in front of me. There wasn't much I'd ever done besides the diner, no kids, no men in my life to speak of, but I know how to cook breakfast and lunch. I figured I'd put up a big sign that said *Free Biscuits Monday 6-8 A.M.* Even when I came up with the idea, the hands stayed around. So then I guessed they were here for some other reason and ever since they've stayed right in view off to the left a bit. Even now when I have flour going every which way they're floating there pretty as a picture.

I wanted something nice for the sign, not some chicken-scratch like I normally do when I run a special. One thing Momma was always sad about was how Desdemona got into college and I got the backbone for restaurant work. I went up to Fole's Electrical and Sign because Clarence owed me a basket-full of biscuit favors. Clarence is an old-timer around Blue Falls, too. But he hasn't lost his stamina. He keeps up and ahead of his son, rewiring houses and painting signs. The only thing now is that he wears jump suits on account of his surgery. Still stands tall as ever, though. And his eyelids droop down slightly and so sweetly over his eyes. I told him to fix up a nice sign on a sandwich board that I could set out on the sidewalk. I asked him if he could do that and he just said "Yep." I thanked him and he walked me to the door. "Real nice day," he said.

"I guess so," I said back. I had so much on my mind that I hadn't even taken notice. We had one of those cool, cloudless days you get only up here. The kind where the sun seems like a bright thumbtack holding up the whole sky. Then I noticed those hands pressed tightly together. I wondered if Clarence saw them, but he never said anything and I was afraid they'd poof away if I said a word so I just shut up.

Clarence scuffed a bit and then spoke. "I'm going down to Bonneville in a few days to walk around the dam if you care to see it." Clarence used to work under Daddy at the dam but I'd never been there in all these years.

"That's a nice offer," I told him, "but I've got a bunch of work to get done before Monday."

He shook his head and the hands were praying extra seriously. "Maddy," Clarence said, "let Patrick run the diner for a day."

You have to understand this came out of nowhere, this asking me to go off to Bonneville which is just down the road a bit, but still. Clarence has been widowed nearly four years. Connie was a sweet woman. About as thin as I am filled out. And her hands were tiny as a squirrel's. But she could sew up a storm. Made quilts and sold them out of Clarence's shop. Now and then Blue Falls gets a tourist that wants to go out to the bridge, and if they stopped in town when Connie was alive, sure enough they'd leave with one of those quilts. But in all this time Clarence hasn't asked me to do a thing. Come to think of it, it isn't too often that I see him when he isn't having breakfast on my counter. So I kind of glanced over my shoulder to see if those hands were going to be any help, and of course they weren't. They just stayed there praying. So I said yes and we set a time.

Right about now is when I wish those hands would pitch in. Rolling out biscuit dough you can't be too rough and you can't throw too much flour on to keep it from sticking to your board or rolling pin. Better to have a bit of sticking than dry old dough. And I'm taking care of everything myself. All these years I've been saying I could use an extra pair of hands and here they are and they don't do anything but float and pray. They don't show much use for what I thought they came for either, which was to get this meeting off right.

One thing's for sure, even after all these years, I like the diner best early in the morning. I have just enough light to see by and everything's calm and kind of dark yellow. Maybe these empty seats remind me that I'm all alone, but I also try to tell myself about how good I've done since Daddy died, since Desdemona left, since Momma died. And I got the oven warming up beside me and I know people are coming in a few hours. So I go about getting my potatoes and onions chopped if I haven't done it the day before. Put on some coffee and make sure all the syrups, sugar, salt and pepper, and ketchup are filled. And all these things start mixing together in some kind of sweet smell and I get to feeling hopeful and anxious to see who'll be in.

This morning I mostly have to tend to the biscuits. Patrick set up everything else yesterday. But the biscuits are enough to take care of because I'll be giving those away for free. Free for the price of listening to what I have to say about this company coming in and leveling Blue Falls. They figure in a year they can have most of town torn away and replaced. It makes me miserable thinking about it. Maybe that's why I went ahead and spent the day with Clarence last week. Just to take some time not thinking about it. Because I know that whatever I come up with to say isn't going to make much difference if people see dollar signs in their heads.

Clarence was very sweet. He brought me the signboard for the meeting, all done in big blue letters, clear as a dime in a water pail. He set it up right in front of the diner and stood back with his hands perched on the hips of his gray jump suit. "What do you think?" he said. I smiled and told him it looked very nice. Better than I could've imagined. Then we were off to Bonneville in his pickup to look at the dam. And those hands were there too. Except, instead of sitting over my shoulder they were right in the middle of the dashboard next to the plastic Jesus. If you don't think there's something uncomfortable about seeing a pair of praying hands right next to a statue of Jesus while you're going down the road, then I don't know what.

Clarence isn't one for much talk but he seemed pretty talkative for him. "What're you going to say when you give away those biscuits?" he asked me.

"Don't know," I said. And that was the truth. Still is.

"Well I'm with you, old gal," he said. And that's what he called me but I didn't take offense. I guess I am an old gal.

We were pretty much quiet the rest of the way, which isn't too far. Of course it was the best part of the year. Halfway between spring and summer, so everything's about as new green as it can get. And if you stand and be quiet you can hear the air. I'm not talking about the wind. I'm saying if it's perfectly still, the air makes a real tiny sound like someone whispering, only you can't make out words, but you understand anyway. Of course, in the truck we were whizzing by everything. There isn't a person in town that doesn't watch out for Clarence's driving. Of course, he isn't ever late either.

He's a good man. A worker. You can see it in his hands. He doesn't even have to grip the steering wheel tight at all because they're so strong. The only thing is the nails are bitten back to the nub. And the strange part is he suddenly doesn't wear his wedding ring anymore. I saw that right off when we got in the truck. That's another thing I'm not going to talk about. But it doesn't take much to figure out I've thought Clarence was very handsome right from the time I met him all those years back. I never said a word because he had just gotten married when Daddy moved us here and then Connie and I ended up friends. But Clarence is the only man in Blue Falls I've ever given a second thought to in that way.

So Clarence is normally very quiet, like I said, but he straightened up a bit like he was going to say something important. "You ever hear from Desdemona?"

That was the last thing I expected him to say. "I *never* hear from Desdemona and I don't expect I really want to."

"Now, Maddy," Clarence said to me just like Daddy used to, "she's your only sister and you aren't getting any younger. Don't you think you ought to patch things up?"

As much as I care for Clarence, I didn't need to hear him tell me about my own sister and I said so. Desdemona left us and I hardly hear from her except maybe once a year. She's always off to one country or another, doesn't even have a home address that I know of. I write her at the university if I want to get ahold of her. Whatever ties we had she gave up as far as I'm concerned. That may sound rock-ribbed, but I don't mean to. I know Momma never gave up on her. And when we were girls you couldn't fit a toothpick between us, we were so close. I remember around the time Desdemona started to develop the Turner boys were giving her a hard time every day after school. We figured out a way for her to lead them through our orchard so I could ambush them with some green apples to the head. The older one, Jacob, walked around for days with a big pink welt square in the middle of his forehead. He told everyone it was from playing baseball. Of course, Desdemona and I straightened that out real quick.

But things changed between me and Desdemona when she found those bones of that surveyor from the 1800s. It was an accident, but the newspapers made a big deal of it and she had that scholarship waiting for her when she graduated high school. After that she was pretty much not my sister anymore. She got lost in her books and in that *National Geographic* subscription Momma bought her. Then she went to college and that's about it. I told Clarence all that and added that I didn't need him to remind me I wasn't getting any younger. "I have a mirror that tells me the same thing every morning," I said.

The whole ride those hands sat on the dashboard praying and I can't say I wasn't getting a little irritated with the whole thing. What were they praying for anyway? I'm not one to look back and regret too much, but right then I was thinking about how maybe my life would have turned out different. If I was to do it all over again, maybe I might've married and had some kids. Maybe I wouldn't have had to work so hard with the diner and taking care of Momma. Right about now I'd be having little ones calling me Grandma and that wouldn't be too bad. And I might have made sure I knew where Desdemona was all the time. I guess right then I was wishing I could wipe the whole slate clean. Level it all and start over. I didn't turn out bad, perhaps, just not as good as I could have.

But I can't be dwelling on all that again even if it's true. There's too much to get done yet. The oven should be ready about now. Most people have sloppy ovens and that won't do if you have something to bake. I don't mean dirty, either. A little grease here and there never hurt a soul. But you have to watch the temperature. Momma used to cook on a wood stove back in Missouri and she'd watch the thermometer very carefully. She knew how to add a stick or two to raise the temperature and everything always came out perfect. She made a gooseberry cobbler that I haven't tasted better of since.

So in ovens like we have now, you'd figure people would pay attention, but I can't say how many burned cakes or doughy muffins I eat and I just shake my head. This morning I have my ovens set right at 425 and they run right to the degree, too. People always complain they can't make biscuits like me, but truth be told, I bet they haven't bothered to check their ovens. Carpenters don't work with broken hammers. Preachers don't preach without the Bible. But everyone sure expects to bake with sloppy ovens.

It'll be light pretty soon and Patrick'll be in and I haven't figured out what to say. I look at those hands but they aren't any help.

"What are you doing here anyway?" I ask, but nothing comes back. You'd think they'd know sign language or something. But I guess that wouldn't do much good either because I wouldn't understand what they were saying anyway. It would be nice to know what they were praying on though. It's like having someone knock on your door one day and you invite them in and they don't say a word. Just stare at you. But I know they're up to something. They have to be. Maybe when people come in and I'm talking they'll turn into a whole body and say that they came to save Blue Falls. But when I think about that, I can't make my mind up whether it'd be a man or a woman standing there. You can't tell from looking, but I haven't ever seen a man pray as much as those hands.

Now that I think of it, I suppose I have seen a praying man. Clarence used to be religious before his wife died. He even substituted a couple times when the preacher went to Seattle to take care of his folks. But Clarence doesn't do much praying now. I don't know that he turned away from God so much as he just doesn't make a big show of it anymore. But he's still sweet. I can't think of a better day I've spent than when the two of us and those hands went to the dam. I had no idea Daddy worked in such a big place. And they let us walk the whole place by ourselves. Waved at us, and all of them knew Clarence by name. First he took me down underneath until he said we were below water level and I could barely hear him above the sound of the turbines. And all they got for light are ordinary old bulbs. If anything ever looked like it was about to spring a leak, it was all that concrete around us. There wasn't a bolted place that wasn't crusted up with lime.

I felt a lot better up top. They have a man-made salmon run

but the salmon don't come upstream this time of year so Clarence took me over to the locks and we saw the Kelsons in their boat going downriver. They've lived in Blue Falls about fifteen years. Good folks even if they are from California. They've done a lot for the town, that's for sure. Got the county to fix the roads. Dick can talk your ear off and I suppose he jaw-boned the county until they got tired of hearing him complain and gave up and put in some new asphalt. The Kelsons got a very pretty daughter too, Jordan. One time she came into the restaurant and I was shorthanded and she stayed the whole morning busing tables.

So Clarence and I watched those heavy gates open up and the Kelsons boat slip in and the gate close behind them. I called down as loud as I could when the water was lowering and asked if they were coming to the meeting. "Wouldn't miss it, Madeleine," Dick said. "We're going down with the ship, too, Captain." He gave me a kind of salute. Then they were out the other gate and Clarence brought me over to the side of the dam and, darned if right in one of the intakes there wasn't the biggest log I ever seen. It was about as wide across as a man from head to foot. Clarence called it a rogue. Said that happens once in a while and he had a few unrepeatable words for how much trouble it was to get those pulled out. Right then a breeze came up and I noticed something. My hair went every which way but those hands stayed right in one place in front of me. So I reached out again like when I first saw them and I didn't feel a thing. Then I ran my hand between them and the sun and my shadow didn't hit them. They stayed that same bright brown. Clarence asked me if something was wrong. I suppose I looked like a crazy woman. "Nothing," I told him and I tried to smile.

Clarence and I had a fine day. We had a bite to eat in Bonneville and then we drove up to Pewter Lake so Clarence could
catch a few squawfish to bury in his garden. He had two poles
and some red wigglers in the back of the pickup, so I felt good
knowing he planned to spend the whole day with me.

It was near dark when we got to the lake, which is high this
time of year. We sat up on the rocks and cast our lines. Then Clarence took out a couple beers and we settled into catching some fish.
But I guess I wasn't paying too much attention to the fishing.
Looking out across the lake I saw the house lights coming on all
over the hillsides just as pretty as Christmas trees. I was looking at
practically all the families left in Blue Falls. So many people have
gone off. Lots of those to Los Angeles for some reason. But I was
thinking about the families that stuck it out. How they'd be having
dinner and then doing the dishes. Maybe they'd watch the TV.
Maybe their kids would be doing homework on the kitchen table.
It's the kind of thinking that makes you feel happy and alone at the
same time. I looked at those hands next to me hoping they
understood what I did and that all that praying they were doing
would come to some good. And I came to my own decision that
when I got back I'd write Desdemona and say I needed her home
for a bit. Looking out at Blue Falls made me realize I should see her
before we both got too old to appreciate each other.

"We have a real nice town," I said to Clarence.

"Sure do," he said back to me. "Hope people listen to you."
Then he took a long gulp of beer and looked at me and kind of
laughed. "You're our Moses."

Maybe it was the beer or maybe I just felt comfortable, but I stood up with my pole in my hand like Charlton Heston in that movie. "Let my people stay," I said and Clarence started laughing again. Then I raised my arms and told him I was going to part the waters of Pewter Lake and we had a good laugh over that too. We were having a nice time. Then squawfish started finding our bait, so we were busy pulling in fish and drinking beer and I forgot every worry I had.

I guess that day with Clarence was one of the best I ever spent in all the years I've lived here. I know some people can go a whole lifetime and never make a friend like him. So now that I think of it, maybe I wouldn't want to start my life over from scratch. I suppose you couldn't do that anyway and what good would come of it? Even if things are downright awful, there isn't any such thing as really starting over. You just have to look around and make what you have the best you can. Maybe what I have to say this morning to folks is as simple as that. If they think things are going to be better after those bulldozers come in and flatten everything down for a hotel they're mistaken. There's plenty good about Blue Falls, mostly the people, and a lot of us have forgotten that. It isn't an inspirational speech but I can't think of a truer thing I might say.

So I finally come up with some words and none-too-soon because my hands are about give out and the door'll be open soon. But I'll keep going. I always do. I have a lot of biscuit-making days ahead of me but like I said before, it isn't too hard a thing to imagine I might walk back home one of these times and lay my head down just like Momma did when she took ill. And maybe there won't be anyone to sit by me and run their fingers through my hair but that won't mean it wasn't a good life.

Now I look at those hands floating as steady and prayerful as always and I think I have them figured out. They were praying all this time for me to find the right words to tell Blue Falls and I guess I have. Seems like now they might disappear or something but they're still here, maybe just for companionship, even as I'm cutting out the last of the biscuits, and all of it feels right. We spend so much of our lives stiff-arming the world until we realize that what a person needs is a feeling there's someone or something watching out for them. And that's just where I have to start today when I give my talk. At the same time I'm going to say that maybe we don't examine ourselves in the mirror enough and ask Who am *I* looking out for? I guess my answer's walking through the door this morning—times a couple dozen people. And just thinking about that is enough to keep a body from feeling alone. But before all that, before the clacking of plates and silverware, before all the commotion, it's just me and those hands and the diner and everything's perfectly quiet.

White Hand

—||||||||—

"I t's a good day for Ching Ming," my father pronounces as if he has chosen this particular sun and vapor-streaked sky. The heated L.A. wind flashes up the hillside as my father looks out, his heavy black hair flailing up, revealing his high forehead. This year, Ching Ming and the opening day of baseball have fallen on the same date. Today, Chinese people honor their dead and Americans officially come out of hibernation. The outfield walls of Dodger Stadium are looped with red, white, and blue bunting, and Forest Lawn cemetery is dotted with clusters of Chinese families holding bouquets of purple iris and bright delphinium mixes. The air is filled with a momentum of contradictions pulling my father and me in opposite directions.

I feel the gap widening and my father forming words I do not want to hear. He is satisfied with the view from Yeh Yeh's grave, on a hill looking at a panorama I cannot comprehend—the San Fernando valley, Chinatown, Los Angeles, and finally the Pacific. Though nothing is distinct, it's enough he knows what fills the vast space in his sight. "I don't think you will understand today," he says to me. "This is very Chinese."

"I know what we're doing." I turn to my father's Chinese wife, Paula, who is holding the hand of Di-gooma—literally meaning eldest sister of my father. She keeps a small space between herself and Paula, who is rolling her eyes at something my father says in Chinese. She looks at me and then my father, shaking her head in frustration, and she gestures to me not to worry. Of course, he is not paying attention to her. Though my mother is German-Irish I see a great deal of her in Paula. I see my father's type. She holds her shoulder-length hair away from her face with a butterfly clip, broadening her perfect smile, something my mother doesn't have.

My father says Paula is vanilla Chinese. By this he means a woman who grew up in the Chinese community in Monterey Park, a suburb with boxy tract homes and thirty-year-old juniper invading lawns and sidewalks. You do not see adults on the streets there, my father says, only children biking to violin lessons or, on Saturdays, to Chinese school. Paula has told me about her teacher, Mrs. Chang, who kept a tin of salty plums for her students. Though my father complains Paula neglects her heritage, I can't help thinking of two things that run in her favor: She looks the part of a Chinese wife and she acts like my mother.

My father speaks in Cantonese to Di-gooma and she agrees

without looking at him. Paula is nodding her head. Even though I don't speak Chinese, I assume a translation and nod too. The day is warm and rare. The wind has blown the haze away, leaving behind a surprising amount of color. The seventy-year-old pines are dense with a deep wool green that contradicts the bright grass, cut short like a quick infield. It is easy to believe at the center of all this is Pak Yuan-zhong's grave.

We are not solemn. That season has passed and now we simply observe a duty. "You didn't have to meet us," my father says to me.

"If you can drive up from San Diego, I can drive ten minutes."

"Your studies. You are usually so busy."

Did he intend that? Was it another reference to Ma Ma? Six years ago they celebrated her eightieth birthday. All the grandchildren went except me, my father's only child. "A great insult," he had said. I never understood if that meant to him or my grandmother. I was two hundred miles away preparing for midterms. My father doesn't see his contradictions. He has never let me celebrate his birthday. "It's not important," he told me. "Americans waste too much time on birthdays." If he had said "This is important," I would have been at Ma Ma's. Should I have known automatically? Is that Chinese?

"What is that supposed to mean?" I finally say. "You know I make an effort to participate in this family."

"It should not be an effort," he replies, folding his arms. That is it.

All I can think of is the video of Ma Ma's birthday, my cousins getting up to a small podium and saying in various form—I love you, Ma Ma. I wish you good health. Then my father got up and read the note I sent already translated for me into Chinese. I had read a book of Tang poems to make my pen wise in a language I didn't speak. I told my father to open the envelope only when it was his turn. His reading sounded violent. "We are only enlightened if we outlive the myths of our youth and savor the truth in our age. Ma Ma, I admire you for being such a person." My relatives nodded and smiled but my father put the note back in the envelope and stuffed it in his jacket.

"I'm never too busy for the important things," I say, trying to salvage the moment. "Where are Yee and Yuan and the others? Am I the only grandchild coming today?" Listening to my words, I imagine my English changes when I speak to my father.

"Maybe they are coming later," he offers. "I would not expect them to leave work early. They have good jobs that you cannot just leave when you feel like it."

"I gave up Dodger tickets to be here. Opening day."

"Games and work are not the same," he snaps. "You are too much like your mother."

"Are you two going to argue all afternoon again?" Paula interrupts, shaking her head at both of us. "We're here for better reasons. Your sister is ready." She leans over and whispers in my ear. "When you two fight, he stays mad for a week."

Di-gooma walks to the front of Yeh Yeh's grave. She makes me nervous because she is always smiling at me with silver-framed teeth. I can't tell if she approves or disapproves because even her expressions seem to be a different language. She is tall for a Chinese woman, with thick hands which have never picked rice or peonies—maybe in the previous generation, in Ma Ma's province, but in San Diego she watches Chinese videos and cooks bad food on her electric range. She is ten years older than my father and her thin hair is gray at the roots where she parts it. Her carpet-thick navy blue pants suit disguises a gender she seems to have forgotten.

Di-gooma bows three times at the waist, allowing her arms to hang straight with gravity. Though I am watching her, I am thinking about being too much like my mother. Twenty-eight years ago, hers were qualities worth marrying for. She told me she and my father met when she was working at Dairy Queen on 30th in San Diego. My father lived two blocks away and came in every day for a vanilla cone. I've seen the pictures. His future had been chosen by Yeh Yeh. He was here on a student visa, a crew-cut business major with a pocket full of pens always in his short-sleeved white shirt. My mother wore sleeveless dresses and kept her henna-streaked hair in a tailored swirl, with sharp bangs. Her eyes are still the flashing color of kerosene. "I was pink bubble gum to your dad," my mother told me. "Gum and pizza, cold Coke, and most of all space. He didn't fall in love with me, he fell in love with not being in Hong Kong with his dad and a few million other people." She will never tell me why she loved him.

Di-gooma's face is now tired and expressionless, like it has contemplated a thousand deaths and come to no conclusion. She says something to my father in Chinese as she steps back from the grave.

"Pak Yuan-zhong, 1911 to 1987," my father reads, stepping up to the grave. "All his grandchildren have gone to college. But he was most concerned that they remember their heritage." He takes off his glasses and holds them in his left hand which is speckled with scars from wok-splatter after years of running his restaurant. He bows three times and allows Paula to repeat the gesture. They stand together as if posed, embroidered over a background of freeways and buildings shimmering in the heated wind like metallic crocus. This is how they stood for the photograph.

My father remodeled Canton Kitchen and was having photos taken with the Kiwanis club for the *San Marcos Register.* I was helping with the grand re-opening. He stood with Paula at the center of the membership. The Kiwanis members looked like seasoned sportscasters, clad in navy blue blazers and red ties. My father wore his chef's outfit and Paula a poly-silk blouse with a cherry-blossom print.

"Would anyone notice if Japanese and Chinese waitresses switched clichés?" I asked Paula.

"My other choice was a water-chestnut and foot-binding print," she said.

But I remember the moment of the picture. The Kiwanis president gave the photographer and my father some last minute instructions. "Now get everyone in. We'll put Mr. Zhong and his wife in the middle." The four rows reformed into tighter lines. The men straightened their ties and jacket shoulders. With their pink skin and prominent bridges between their eyes, any one of them could have been my mother's father or brother. "Come on now," the club president said. "This is like a family picture."

I was standing behind the photographer when I heard this. I looked straight at my father and he looked back at me. I questioned him with a raise of my eyebrows: shouldn't I be included in a "family" picture? The muscles in his face tightened, squaring his jaw. I had seen this look before. It was his sign saying "Do not correct me." He shook his head—imperceptible to anyone but me. No, he was saying, you do not look Chinese. This is business. You do not belong in this picture. I could read all those words in the shake of his head. He managed a proprietor's smile just as the camera flashed.

"What was that all about?" I asked afterward.

"People should think this is a Chinese restaurant. If you are in the picture, customers might think it's not run Chinese. Maybe they think you are the owner and I am the cook."

"As if the world is filled with fifteen-year-old restaurateurs."

"Subconscious. People see Caucasian and they make a judgment. I can't help that."

"It's what *you* know that's important to me. I'm your son."

My father looked at me with still, black eyes that refused to reveal anything. "You question too much," he said. "I never talked back to your Yeh Yeh. And I should have listened to him more. He said I wouldn't finish school. He didn't want me to marry your mother. He said we would divorce." My father stopped talking as if he had been warned from saying the things he meant. "We've got too much to do," my father finished, walking to the back entrance of the restaurant.

We fed the Kiwanians lunch, heavy with beef and salt and the baby vegetables, which seemed exotic to them. This is the art my father mastered: understanding the palette of another culture. The men do not question what they eat because my father learned to use the word "authentic" like one of his spices. The waitresses, a Thai, two Koreans, and Paula, all looked Chinese to dozens of pairs of light eyes. They served course after course on utility China embossed with red dragons and oyster-blue pagodas. I cleaned dishes in the kitchen, washing away a mixture of rice and shrimp tails. As I scraped the leftover food into the disposal I tried to imagine a photograph of people who look exactly Chinese, people born with the traditions inside them.

It is my turn to bow at Yeh Yeh's grave and I am better at it this year. My arms hang just as Di-gooma's had, and my face imitates the respectful sternness lost to her generation. But I am doing something wrong. I am not considering Yeh Yeh.

Kneeling down after I am finished, I begin pulling the grass from around the marker. I am using only one hand. It is an old habit to protect my pitching arm, but the limb concedes what my mind has already; I haven't played baseball in five years.

"We should have done this first," Paula says as she starts to help, her obligatory jade bracelet clacking against the marker. In Chinese she asks Di-gooma to join us. The reply is hoarse and reluctant but obedient. The skin on their arms and faces shines in the sun like a deep aloe—a warm, diluted copper.

As we reveal the outer bevels of Yeh Yeh's grave my father stands over us, focusing on the work of our hands. His back is to the sun, making his face dark and simplified. It is the lack of features which captures me, cheeks raised with the round smoothness of melon, and a nose like a polished shell drifting up between his eyes into a mere suggestion of a bridge. Sometimes we forget the exactness of the features of those closest to us, but suddenly I remember this one from my past. Just now, my father looks younger and it's a face I have not seen since I was a child. He's wearing an expression both familiar and distant. Suddenly, the day of the story occurs to me, a source of erosion, perhaps.

It was one of the weekends after the divorce. My mother brought me to our front door where my father waited outside. "No red meat," she said in delayed response to my meal accounts from the previous weekend.

"Did you hear that?" he said. "No monkey this time." I laughed in my sharp nine-year-old's voice.

That time, like once every month, we planned a trip to the San Diego Zoo for my requisite stop beneath and beyond the dark archway of the Reptile House. As soon as we walked through the turnstiles, I started running toward the snakes but my father called to me and I stopped, knowing what we were in for. Before anything else, we had to visit the flamingo lagoon. I complained with the exaggerated gestures I could get away with at my age. I flung my arms to my side and sagged my body into an angle of irritation. "You're too impatient," my father said.

The lagoon was really just an ankle-deep, light blue pond framed by lush tree ferns and giant bird of paradise. The flamingos stood tall and still as if they were pink stencils on a postcard. Occasionally one bent its long neck down, shaking its dark beak in the water. "Beautiful," my father said. On our first trips, he lugged a bag of camera equipment around, stopping at every animal. I was glad we were past the photograph stage—the snakes were waiting.

I tugged at my father's arm until he relented and we finally went to the Reptile House. I ran through the dark portal, past all the small glass windows, to the largest exhibit where they kept the pythons. My father stopped at the first window. He was a small silhouette leaning into the glass. As usual, he preferred to read the entire display before moving on to the next reptile. I stayed with the pythons. Their enclosure occupied one corner of the building, leaving room for two picture windows. The remaining walls were lime green, dulled by the fluorescent lights above the gray stones on the floor. One of the other snakes was curled among the perfectly smooth branches in the center. The other snake lay almost completely stretched out near the glass where a line of hand-and-nose smudges marked the visits of children who came before me. The snake was completely still, its scales an intricate inlay of several dark shades of green. This time it had a large lump about four feet from its head. "It's eaten a rabbit," my father said from behind me. I was startled that he had gotten that far so quickly.

"You caught up fast," I said. "How do you know it ate a rabbit?"

My father pointed to the small chalkboard hanging above us. It read, "Ilsa is not pregnant. We fed her a rabbit."

"See what you miss when you do not read," my father said. "Where is the noun in the second sentence?"

"School let out yesterday."

"Give the answer and I will tell a reptile story."

I looked at my father, a little surprised. He had never told me a story before. I read the sign and answered. "Rabbit, I guess."

Pleased with my reply, my father led me to a peanut-shaped bench where we sat down. A thread of sunlight running across his face outlined his rounded features. "Your Yeh Yeh told me this story when we were escaping the Communists," he began.

"In our ancestors' village in Canton, the first of our great-grandfathers put his ear to the ground and heard the footsteps of a dragon. For protection, he gathered all the citizens to dig a huge pit in front of their houses. They worked for seven days, digging until they did not have ropes long enough to climb out of the hole if they dug deeper. Our great-grandfather instructed them to put bamboo spikes at the bottom and cover the top with every kind of bush and tree.

"When they finished, Great-grandfather sent them home and he sat at the edge to wait. The moon and the sun sat at the opposite horizons. The dragon approached and the ground shook so badly Great-grandfather felt he might fall into the hole himself. The dragon's own breath created a thick, hot fog so that our great-grandfather could not see him at first. Then he saw the dragon's great body emerge through the mist on the other side of the trap. The dragon's head was thin and long with a great split tongue lashing out of it. Scales a thousand times larger than a python's covered his body—bright green on the top and yellow on his belly. His large red eyes spotted Great-grandfather, who taunted the dragon. All the villagers came out and cheered our great-grandfather. They covered the dragon with dirt except for its back which curved above the top of the pit. Even today there is a mound in our ancestors' village marked by the dragon's spine, which petrified into a line of boulders."

My father finished his story, smiling as if he had given me a precious gift. Today, cleaning Yeh Yeh's grave, it is that smile that comes back to me so clearly. I see my father's face waiting for a response—and myself as a boy not reading the signs, thinking about the other corners of the Reptile House, the anacondas and monitor lizards. "There are no such things as dragons," I said, hopping off the bench, leaving my father behind.

We are almost finished picking the grass away. "What now?" I say to my father. He turns and looks at the view again, holding his hands behind his back. He gives a few short nods as he has always done before making a point. "I wish you could understand what we do," he says to me.

"I could tell you he means well," Paula says to me quietly, trying to translate my father's ambiguity. "But I don't know what he means."

"My son plays Chinese," he continues. "Today is Ching Ming, he thinks, so he will be Chinese. Look at him—at his confusion. His eyes have no single color, his hair is dark but swirls from his scalp. And where is my skin? Even this would not concern me if it did not go all the way through. But I understand this because I married his mother."

Paula sizes up my father and me. He stares directly at me and I feel the tenseness in my jaw. "Right now you two look at each other like you're about to meet combat," Paula reprimands.

"Why don't you give me credit for trying," I say, realizing the weakness of my words.

He turns fully toward us. "Maybe I am warning. You cannot turn Chinese on and off. I tried to be Chinese. I cut my hair prickly short. Your mother taught me how to dance American. We listened to Aretha Franklin and watched *Ed Sullivan*."

As he speaks, I think of how, at night, the television makes my mother's white skin glow blue, how she sits with her legs curled up on the couch. I wonder if this is how my father remembers her. "What does that have to do with me?" I ask.

"Often I would leave my studies and go to her apartment to eat ice cream she brought home from work," he says. "I would do this even on nights I knew your Yeh Yeh was going to call from Hong Kong.

"I never told him about your mother. When I announced we were getting married he was so startled he said only, 'Is this girl pregnant?' Then, he was silent. It was poor timing for me to also tell him I was on academic probation. More bad grades and I would be dismissed from school. 'So you get married?' he yelled. This made me nervous even though he was across the Pacific. 'I could have one of your cousins talk to the school. Or Dr. Tongqi.'

"'I'm going to be married,' I said to him.

"'You cannot know her well. Does her family come from mainland recently? Do they speak Chinese or only English?'

"Of course he assumed she was Chinese. When I answered his questions there was only the static of long distance between us and then he quietly hung up. Later, he predicted the ruin of my marriage, but just then he was using the phone again to warn my relatives away from our wedding. Your mother's family did not come either." My father stops and considers this for a moment, checking my face to see if I understand the implications. I feel as if he is unloading stones from an invisible sack slung over his shoulder.

"I did not speak Chinese for two years," he continues. "The first words I spoke again in my own language came when I called my father to tell him about his grandson. He answered the phone and I said 'Pa-pa' and waited for him to respond.

"He said, 'You must raise him Chinese.'

"I had almost forgotten how to be Chinese myself. You cannot wear culture like a costume. You must feel the history in your blood. Today, you honor Yeh Yeh, but he is all you know. I watch you clean his grave and I worry that your China is only a dish I serve." My father stands, unmoving, at the rim of a chasm dug by his ancestors, waiting for me.

There are too many bamboo spikes in this hole, I think. This is only the second time my father has extended himself, only it's not a story. I can't just walk away.

I am already thinking of China and its wall that can be seen from outer space. I imagine the pale gray birds perched on its stones. I see my father and me walking there alone, the birds lighting off into the morning, into mist and green trees and the soft clash of leaves in a calm breeze. He tells me about this country of colors and about its millenniums. I am a tourist.

Di-gooma and Paula stand up and let me pluck the remaining vegetation around the grave. The back of my neck is hot and stung by the sun. I am pulling at individual blades of grass even though the brass marker is completely revealed. Today is Ching Ming. There is no conversation or wind or sound. We are all watching my hand moving, picking, doing way too much, beyond what has been asked and what will be appreciated—a hand, white, so white against the gravesite of Yeh Yeh, Grandfather.

Leases

———|||||||———

T his is the time of morning to choose names for babies that
will never be born. It is easy to imagine the beginning of
some brash alteration, that just beyond Larkin's reach, the air is
lavender in the dim early light. Vision is an obsolete sense as his
feet carry him along the concrete walkway and he is guided by the
nearly suppressed smell of jasmine. It is winter in Los Angeles and
these are its shades. Sparrows rock a hibiscus, its yellow trumpet
of petals rashed with color that might be the maroon of rusted
keys or burned out stars. The leaves are bright from the morning
dampness, a waxy green refraction.

This is my element, Larkin thinks. I could walk into the air,
take an implausible direction.

The apartment building is indistinct, a void or passageway. Larkin adjusts the flattened cardboard boxes under his arm and feels for his keys. He has not been here in a week and the small porch is littered with restaurant flyers and coupons for car washes and neighborhood markets. They are like black ribbon or wreaths on the door, progressive signals of vacancy, a seal he wishes Ona could see. He knew she was serious when she asked him to terminate the rental and he agreed, though as he turns the lock, he understands nothing has been decided.

He stands in the open doorway and lights a cigarette. The living room is cast noir like intermission lights on an open stage. The taste is not his, though he paid for everything, the retro Formica dining-room set, the squat lima-green sectional curving around a boomerang-shaped coffee table. Over the years, the men he brought here added these touches, the mustard wall in the bedroom, deco sconces. They all found ways to leave their marks. The only item of Larkin's is a six-foot wall-hanging of green and red caladiums.

Tomorrow is his and Ona's anniversary, and this morning is Larkin's gift to her. He has asked her to meet him here after she finishes consulting at Santa Monica Bay. He is unprepared for what he has promised, a kind of euthanizing beyond giving up men. In his forty-seventh year he is not sure if this act of regression is possible. He views his life as a product of occupations. Ona is an oceanographer, studying the forces of shore erosion, and he has traveled the world as an engineer. When they were on the border of Spain for one of Larkin's jobs, Ona was ill and stayed in the hotel, deciding on variations of *Renee* for their first child. "You build a dam," she said. "A few years later they hire me to tell them why there's no sand on the beach."

The memory has a liquid quality to Larkin, clear as vermouth. "If you stop the rivers, you change the sea," she said. By how many fractions has he altered the earth, Larkin wonders, and what acts of sabotage has Ona imagined from her bed?

Larkin has come to pack but there is no single thing he wants to take with him. He sets the boxes he's holding just inside the front door. How many men had he brought here when the morning had given up its nature to the heat of concrete and stucco? Sometimes he would respond to an ad, hear a voice, and then sit in this same room waiting for a knock, not knowing who might walk through the door. Most of the men were only invited here once, but some of them he liked, perhaps could have shared a life with; the one from Washington state who had the thick sweetness of burning olive wood, and the other who asked to move in. Under different circumstances he might even have introduced them to Ona. But he always locked an empty apartment and drove home. Larkin remembers how everything seemed tainted afterward, freeways sluggish as collapsed veins, the livid taste of ash infiltrating his lungs.

Larkin flicks his cigarette across the small room into the kitchen sink, the light catching the brownish glow of his wedding band. He and Ona used two paychecks to purchase their rings. When they were married, each band rested perfectly round and polished on a satin pillow. Now, his conforms to the shape of his finger and bears a few small scratches. Their wedding guests printed suggestions for their firstborn on a large sign. They ranged from the ordinary like *Joseph* and *Steve* to those playing off the last name *Baum;* *Deactivated* and *Adam*. That was the day the names began. Ona had the sign framed and keeps it even now.

Her image comes to Larkin, the wide smile and the lines around her eyes that he has watched with comfort. Ona is who I contracted to grow old with, he thinks. But like a fog, the scent of the apartment invades, the smell of snuffed-out cigarettes, sex, becomes tangible like some addictive powder.

Larkin opens a window. Street workers are trimming eucalyptus away from the power lines. Perhaps another month, Larkin thinks. He could tell Ona he is leaving, that he doesn't love her. But even as the thought comes to him, he imagines her blue eyes that have begun to turn gray. Figure things out. Whose deadline is it? Maybe there's another way. The smell of cut eucalyptus fills the room, brushing over Larkin light as sky. If I have to choose between two lives, he wonders, why not one with a man?

Ona will be here soon. There are things Larkin planned to say when she walks in the door but he can't recall them. She could do this, he thinks. Ona always knows how to be decisive, cut a deal, move forward. When Larkin's father left him and his mother, it was Ona who got him through it. They were both only fifteen and she was already the strong one. Even this apartment had been her suggestion, a concession that kept him anchored. It is this sureness of Ona at his side that keeps him from drifting away completely.

He feels the damp soil of a potted string-of-pearls passed down from his grandmother. He has started another at home from a cutting. This is one of his and Ona's hobbies, taking field excursions in the neighborhood to ask for stems, cactus stubs, anything that will develop roots. Ona has brought home seeds from the Galapagos and they have a small bromeliad that Larkin found during a water project in the Amazon and which they have named Amy.

He and Ona had cultivated their necessities, considered the difference of grays for the living room, Morning Mist or London-wood. Bristle Fog, or Dove Breast. They coordinated azaleas in the front yard and kept gardening tools outlined in black ink hanging in the garage. Before last year, when Ona quietly told him she had changed and there would be no more choosing names for a baby, there had been the room that remained undone, the one that would never become a nursery; it contained the sewing machine and treadmill. "I've given up enough, Larkin," Ona had said one gray morning.

Daylight is already beginning to take, folding into the room like honey. Larkin looks out the window at the cap of moon in the bluing sky. As a child it seemed so tangibly close he had tied a dozen rolls of string together and asked his father to build a kite big enough to fly into space. He watched the harvest moon rise and wane, close enough, he thought, holding the spool of twine he had wrapped himself. At what point do we define our limits, he wonders. And who teaches us to rescind our aspirations?

There are books on the coffee table that haven't been moved in weeks, a water-damaged copy of *Moby-Dick* and an English anthology next to a sandwich bag with less than a hit of marijuana left inside. Sometimes other men liked to get high but Larkin would not try it. He did not want Ona to smell it on his breath.

In all the years they have been married, he has not seen even a sleeping pill in her medicine cabinet. He has never known Ona to admit pain. It occurs to Larkin that this is a reaction to being married for twenty-nine years, as if she is saving up. They have spent decades eliminating aberration from one another, smoothing their edges the way sacraments subdue with slow erosion into grace and conformity.

The apartment is cool, the air lulled by the prelude of another warm winter day. Larkin steps across the block of light coming from the bedroom door and walks to the kitchen, pulling down a carton of cigarettes and opening a pack. Outside, water drips from the eaves, tapping at the geranium. The constant measure reminds him of Ona getting dressed in the morning, the same drawers lightly closing, the electric click of the closet light, the clasp of a jade bracelet he gave her on their twenty-fifth anniversary. He is comfortable with these sequences. They are part of a private language, a religion of which they are the only practitioners. Their communion has a fluidity.

Larkin turns on the stove, putting a cigarette to his mouth as he bends down to light it in the blue flame. He looks around the apartment, considering what to pack first. He will donate most of the contents, but in the bedroom, there is a torchiere lamp which he will save for Ona. He sits down at the kitchen table, fishing around a silver candy dish but chooses nothing. It is seven-thirty A.M. and his cigarette smoke has turned the air a polished gray. By now, Ona is on her third cup of coffee. He pictures her in the mahogany-trimmed office she designed herself. On important days, when she's not on the ocean, she wears tailored, navy blue suits and gold jewelry. Her blonde hair is pulled back now, secured in a low bun the way her mother wore hers. She gestures politely with white hands, tightening the translucent skin over a lattice of green veins. She has created an order for herself despite him.

The day Ona chose to speak to him about the apartment, she sat Larkin down but continued to stand. "I've never asked you to make choices," she said, "but it's time." There had been a rain the night before and the afternoon sky in the window was blue and lumped with clouds white as birthing cloth. Larkin imagines Ona canceling her appointments and coming home early. She would dash around the house, adjusting furniture that hadn't been used all day, open the side blinds a quarter-inch.

Larkin only now understands the implication of her request. It was a proposal, really, as if they had been separated and it was time to renew their vows. He took her into his arms and they lay on the bed together without speaking, Ona curved into his body, the two of them a pair of cupped question marks. The trees outside layered shadow on the walls, the forms of pine and juniper indistinguishable. Larkin thinks of a world without defined lines and how everything evolves toward precision. Each moment is a genetic tick forward; an obsolete tree dies on a hillside; in certain cities in Portugal, the women no longer pause before speaking.

The apartment is full of light, creating a white expanse. It has the dimensions of a terminal, of arrival and departure. Larkin thinks of the men he has shared these rooms with. Holding a man is like embracing a sack of embers, he decides, the warm skin a thin barrier, their mouths with perfectly set teeth contrasted by the wet pink just beyond.

Larkin moves to the couch, out of habit checking the condition of the sandy brown carpet he has cleaned every two months. He balances an ashtray on his knee, tapping his cigarette on the rim. This apartment is where he discovered he was aware of time the way a mother hears a baby cry before it makes a sound. It was Ona who showed him that true urgency is rare. At first she made him watch an entire sunset. It was a form of withdrawal, seeing the sky evolve into orange, staying until the sun had completely deflated into the Pacific. When she was sure Larkin had learned to stop looking at his watch, Ona took him to Mulholland Drive for the view. That was when they were still occasionally bringing up names for babies. He offered Eva after her mother, and Ona suggested *Justice* if it were a boy. Larkin realizes now, choosing names was their act of consummation.

"How long will you need the apartment?" she had asked.

Larkin was not ready to answer. He held Ona, watching the city, a field of hot coals below the Los Angeles sky offering hardly a star. There are regions where this would be an omen, he thought.

The cigarette smoke is a silver wedge in the light coming through the window. Larkin has no doubt that Ona has tomorrow night's anniversary dinner planned from the first course to waving goodbye. They will hold hands in the driveway until their guests pull away, then walk up the stairs. She will stop at the French doors in the living room, as always, because she likes the view at night when the boulevards divide the city into white fault-lines.

Until today, Larkin has never allowed Ona to come to the apartment. He thinks now he might have kept it private until he moved things out. At first, she jokingly called the apartment his "refuge." He is certain she was trying to make him more comfortable, perhaps let him know she did not consider it a place for sex only. Larkin chose the location because he liked its interior dimensions, a manageable perimeter unlike his home with Ona where every room is so insulated and far-flung it's easy to forget someone else is there. Here, two people can sense each other from every point.

Larkin begins to imagine a life with someone besides Ona. He steps onto the balcony off the living room, settling under the shade of a forty-year-old avocado. With a man there would be no consideration of failed posterity. The days would arrive and pass unburdened by a future. There would be no half-empty rooms to which the doors are always closed like time-locked vaults.

Perhaps this is what Ona is offering now that they will not have children. After all these years, she has become the alternative.

The fog has burned off all the way to the Hollywood Hills. Today, and three or four similar days a year are what people pay for, to be able to see Griffith Park and the huge white letters on the hillside. The best views in Los Angeles are manufactured like extremely clever mattes. It is only because of these, Larkin thinks, that you notice the hills at all. The winter sun heats the earth into mixed fragrances of oil, palm, and everything a damp night has pushed to the ground. It is all rising in unseen columns and Larkin feels it escaping.

The moment is still, as if enveloped in some clandestine hour. He is an audience to light and broken silence. He imagines churches intoxicated with stained glass, and the boats of canals slipping through the water, racing their own images. Children are yelling and running around the courtyard on their way to school and Larkin listens to this aesthetic that Ona already understands. A stiffening breeze rattles the avocado, shaking out sparks of light, hinting at a razorlike blue sky. Larkin does not believe in this solid slate. He looks for possible breaches, doorways into the mesh of indigo atoms. Of course, he decides, the flaw would be to find one.

He walks back into the apartment and takes a chair facing the door. All leases end, Larkin tells himself. Even the sun is temporary. He snuffs out his half-smoked cigarette, stirring the haze he created as he sets the ashtray on the coffee table. He closes his eyes. The hum of the refrigerator gives the apartment a vague pulse. He tries to pinpoint the sound. It is the murmur of a dreaming child, perhaps, or midnight in certain parts of Belize where, he remembers, they extinguish the lamps by hand.

He thinks of the fact Ona has waited for him. She has managed a life despite the division of his own and has issued an invitation. It is a kind of recruitment to finish their lives in pleasant ambivalence. Perhaps when he stands next to her at parties and in theater lobbies he will understand what she has known all along. We spend our energies adjusting the trajectory of our lives. There are paths and names we do not choose, the miscalculations that merge like the tributaries coursing toward a common ocean.

Maybe this is the morning Ona has earned. Larkin considers the formula he has followed, regulating his life like floodgates and spillways relieving the pressure behind a dam. He is a creator of deep bodies of water, lakes straining like bound captives. There is no absolution. By what sequence are a man and woman meant to come together? We are constantly engaged in acts of contrived progression, decoding the confluence of our postures and rituals. And who is to contradict our translations? Larkin looks around his apartment and then directly at the entrance. There could have been someone other than Ona, a man, he thinks, but it is the end of winter in Los Angeles, and she will be the last person walking through this doorway. He watches the L of light coming from the front door, waiting for the inevitable interruption of Ona's shadow. We are caught in a blue improvisation, he thinks, building rooms out of wishes and standing inside our own darkness. And here, in front of the doors, we quietly arrange ourselves, immobilized, watching, praying.

Dog Sleep

———|||||||———

S u Yin had come over at my request. It was the first time she'd been back to the house since the day four months earlier when she filled the minivan with all her clothes, half the bedding, and the toaster oven. But we were working on it. The plan was for her to move back in when Gavin came home from school for the summer. We'd give it one last shot, the three of us a family again. The red lettering on our pagoda mailbox would be true, *The Han Family.*

We sat in the room on the very bed where we conceived Gavin. The air exchanger we'd fought over years earlier moaned in the attic, and our Sharpei, Ritchie, growled and twitched in his sleep in front of us. He was the reason I called Su Yin. This was Gavin's dog. Though we never talked about it, getting Ritchie was a substitute brother for him when we didn't have any more kids. I knew Su Yin would want me to tell her Ritchie was sick. He'd been acting odd for days, eating little, napping a lot. His sad face, more fold and flap than anything else, and his firm torso, made him look like a carnival prize gone wrong.

"He's thin," Su Yin said, bending down next to Ritchie.

She'd lost weight and let her hair grow and I wanted to compliment her but it came out wrong. "You are too," I said.

"I look fine." She rolled her eyes. "What are you feeding him?"

"Rice and lamb like always," I said. I smoothed a wrinkle from my shirt, a new blue oxford I'd bought that afternoon just for Su Yin's visit.

Su Yin stood on her knees, arms at her waist. People thought she was attractive, and she was. I met her in San Francisco at a mutual friend's wedding. She was the only one in pink and she barely spoke English. Su Yin was a Gui Lin girl, broad-cheeked, more angular than most Chinese women. My family had come from outside Nanking. We were short and rounded.

"How does his stool look?" Su Yin asked after watching Ritchie for a while.

"Jesus, I don't know. There's a yard full of it. Be my guest." I gestured broadly to the curtained glass doors and the balcony overlooking our overgrown lawn. I hoped she wouldn't take me up on my offer because she'd find I'd indeed let his shit build up for months.

Su Yin persisted. She put her hand on his head but he did not wake. "Have you taken his temperature?"

"I didn't..." I stopped myself from saying I didn't notice anything wrong until today.

"Of course you didn't." She shook the dog softly and called his name. He slowly rose and gave his stubby tail two meager wags, and then in a wet spurt, farted a rosette of bloody diarrhea onto the wall.

"This is just like with Gavin," Su Yin said. We were standing in our veterinarian's overly bright exam room waiting for her to come in. Ritchie lay between us on the stainless-steel table. "There's another one," Su Yin said, swiping a paper towel at the brownish red mess drooling from Ritchie's anus. She'd gone through a third of a roll since we left the house. Even though she seemed to be keeping up, the dark, bitter smell floated around us. "How long has he been doing this?"

"Today. I mean, just since you saw it at the house." I sat on Dr. Mueller's chair and rolled myself against the wall, palms rubbing my eyes.

"Just like with Gavin," she said again. Our son had wrestled in high school. I took him to all his matches. He was a novelty in our town, a Chinese kid on the mats. But Gavin, always a roundish boy, constantly struggled to make weight. By his senior year he had slipped into a full-fledged eating disorder. When we sent him to therapy for a month, we told people he was at wrestling camp. His recovery over the last year was tenuous, and we both knew it.

"Ritchie was okay yesterday," I said. Su Yin bent over and kissed his forehead, her hair putting a shiny black curtain between me and them. Above her, on the wall, was a large poster advertising a drug for feline HIV. A healthy-looking Siamese sat over the caption *Is he sick?*

"Always too busy. Do you know how many of my concerts you've been to since we married?" Su Yin paused as if I should answer but I knew better. She thrust her hand out showing three strong cellist fingers.

I couldn't argue with her, not even about Gavin. One doesn't choose to be oblivious. My own father never noticed that I was unhappy that he moved us from Hong Kong to Los Angeles. "I'm here with you and Ritchie now," I said, standing up and taking a place next to them.

Su Yin began to cry. She reached into her purse but didn't find what she was after. "What if it's too late?" She looked straight at me, her black eyes bleary with tears. We both turned to Ritchie who was sleeping again. His front paws were moving in the same oddly dainty way he liked to play with his sock toys.

The drive home from the vet was silent. Dr. Mueller told us that Ritchie was suffering from kidney and liver failure. I was relieved it was nothing I'd done. Common in Sharpeis, she said. We'd return in the morning if we wanted to put him down. In the minivan, I sat in the back, Ritchie's head on my lap, Su Yin driving. I knew she would've preferred it the other way around, but she also had a thing about me driving her car. She'd had the seats recovered, I noticed, and the back windows were free from the glaze of Ritchie's drool and snot.

When we pulled up to the house, we didn't get out immediately. It was getting close to twilight. Su Yin sat, looking straight-forward into the brownness of the garage door. I'd seen this view a hundred times with Gavin sitting next to me, still dirty and sweating from soccer or wrestling. I tried to picture where the trajectory of our family had veered. We'd checked off everything on the list like we were supposed to and still there I was, separated with a reeking, dying dog on my lap.

I allowed Ritchie the deep sleep he seemed to be in, his muscles twitching now and then. I wondered what he could be dreaming about. I looked at Su Yin through the rearview mirror. "What are we going to tell Gavin?" I finally said.

"It's his decision." She waited a moment and then turned in the seat to face me. "We can't just put his dog to sleep without telling him."

The vet said that even though he didn't show it, Ritchie was in a lot of pain. She was surprised we didn't follow her advice and put him down right then. At that moment his sleep was partly due to medication. I thought of Gavin and Ritchie playing in the backyard. "It's such an American thing to have a dog," I said. "Back in our village, Papá let me have a pet chicken. We couldn't keep any pet that didn't take care of itself. I raised it from a chick. I called it Yinyin."

"We just had a fish tank," Su Yin said.

"After about a year, Papá killed the chicken and served it at a wedding."

I'm not sure what that meant to Su Yin, but she nodded her head as if I'd said something meaningful. "We're putting Ritchie to sleep in the morning. I'll call Gavin and tell him something."

"The truth?"

"I'll see what kind of mood he's in."

I nodded, and then repeated our objective in my mind. We were putting Ritchie to sleep. It sounded odd to me, "sleep." He was already sleeping. We got out of the van and carried Ritchie into the kitchen, where we set up some bedding and where we could confine him so he didn't leak all over the house if he got up. But there was little chance of that. He was out of it.

After we got Ritchie settled, we each had a cup of tea, Su Yin leaning against the refrigerator facing him, me crouched on a slightly wobbly footstool. Su Yin kept her eyes on the dog, the steaming cup clutched near her chin.

"It's too bad he won't be around for the summer," I said.

Su Yin shook her head for a few seconds, softly clicking her tongue. "Gavin will understand."

"You can stay the night if you want."

She set down her cup and I began to stand but she put her hand out as if she was halting traffic. "I know I can," she said. "You sit with him for a while. Call me if he gets worse. I'm going home to call Gavin." She tapped my cheek, the first physical contact we'd had since we separated, but it didn't feel like love.

I listened as the front door softly clicked shut, and the minivan started up. It groaned in the driveway for minutes. I thought at first Su Yin was coming back in. I waited. Then I wondered if maybe she wanted me to go out to her. I got to the window in time to see her backing out, the headlights lancing the hedges as she curved away, my thin reflection appearing in the glass. I was overdressed. My new shirt came off first and I kept taking off clothes until I was down to my underwear and black socks.

I returned to the kitchen where Ritchie lay on his side, engulfed by the bedding as if he were a terra-cotta statue we'd half unpacked. His paws were moving again and he huffed a muted bark. I sat again on the stool trying to ignore the small paunch of my naked belly. I watched Ritchie for a long time, his eyes closed but twitching. He might have been dreaming about lots of things, a ball, a bird, a knock at the door. But I hoped he was dreaming about a time I could barely remember, when Su Yin was home and before Gavin got sick, when we sat in the backyard on lawn chairs and watched our son and Ritchie play tug-of-war with an old towel. I hoped he was dreaming about those times and I hoped he would keep dreaming all night, because in the morning, we'd go to the vet and put him to sleep. And we'd word it just that way because we never say what we really mean.

Fire Walk:
An Old-Fashioned AIDS Story

———||||||||———

Gideon dials slowly, leaning against the wall of his empty kitchen. He closes his eyes, allowing everything around him to fall away. The ringing on the other end of the phone sounds like the reverberation of a hammer on nails. When it stops, his mother is on the line. Gideon takes a breath of the warm autumn air.

She waits silently—and he says, finally, "Mother, it's time. I've gone as far as I can go."

It will take her three hours to arrive from San Diego. Gideon walks into the living room with its picture windows allowing the late morning light to intensify the white of the now barren walls. In the corner stands a vacuum. It has become a kind of urn, sucking up the large gray flakes falling from Gideon more frequently now. He uses it to remove the evidence of his presence from the dark upholstery of his chairs and most recently has begun running the hose down his arms to the tips of his dry, opaque fingers. "Death by evaporation," he tells friends. The treatments are over. His illness is no longer a dismissible visitor but has, in fact, become his primary companion.

After the final hospital stay, Gideon removed the photographs from the walls of his home and now sits himself among them, chilled by a thin band of air hovering above the oak floor. He considers the photos an index of his life. There are the baked-porcelain framed pictures of friends with red reflecting eyes at parties, and a trip in 1988 to Brazil for a television project. A single black-and-white of a little girl rests in a small gold-plated frame, the only picture his family has of an aunt he never met. The photos of himself record the high cheekbones and sepia-toned skin inherited from his mother. He feels as if he is viewing a former lover. The appeal or even chance of posterity is some hectic blue gesture like a last affair.

He picks up a single 5 X 7, stepping over the piles of photos. Someone will want the frames, he thinks. The redwood chaise on the sun deck is not facing exactly as he prefers but he seldom bothers with this kind of correction anymore. Most of the flowers in his backyard have died back, but seven white roses remain, clustered together like the flared underside of a Spanish skirt. When it is clear, he can see the Hollywood sign on his right and downtown Los Angeles on the left. But it is one of those windless days when the air is imperfectly still and embalmed with a white haze, leaving the impression of something vacant and ruined you expect to come upon at the equator. Gideon has this sense more often now, of a failed civilization offering the invention of time and then surrendering under the force of the millennium it created.

He considers the 5 X 7 of the family reunion nine months earlier sent to him by his mother. The photograph was taken on the porch of his mother's white dairy house in San Diego—five rows, eight and ten across, of women in pink and green pastel sundresses and men folding their thick brown arms across their chests or using them to pull someone closer. His mother was frozen in a laugh, her black hair scrunched back in a pencil-secured bun, enhancing his resemblance to her. She was leaning on his Uncle Stan. One of her hands rested on his stomach, the other held a rifle by its barrel. She had come out of the kitchen spinning the weapon, walking across the wood porch when his uncle grabbed her. "Soak that apron in a pot of hot water," he said, "and we'll all have soup." And then the picture.

Gideon notices in the photograph for the first time that his mother is looking at him in the front row, reclined across the laps of several of his cousins. It is that kind of search done in large groups when seeking the connection of an intimate. Had she caught his eye? He remembers avoiding her most of the day. He entertained his relatives as they always expected, but stayed away from her. Gideon wonders, looking at his glassy hands, if he had been doing the same thing all along. The doctor's best estimate was two months, the ironically phrased deadline which had at last convinced him to ask his mother to come get him.

He has gotten out of Los Angeles just twice since he moved

into this house he used to keep for guests. The first time he left was for his father's funeral, and the second for the reunion in the El Monte valley in San Diego. He left for his mother's house two days before the reunion to help her prepare. He drove down Interstate 5, cutting along the edge of the Pacific at six A.M. It was the only time he had seen this ocean when it was not remarkable to him. Fog the color of lead hung tight above the quelled water, releasing infrequent spots of light. He felt superstitious.

Gideon pulled off the freeway at San Onofre and got out of his car. He was close enough to hear waves manipulating the sand. Leaning on the open door of his car, he allowed his face to collect a mist which felt as cold and sharp as metal shavings. He considered the indefinite shore and this fifth year in which he had gone beyond positive. The apocalypse has fooled us all, he thought. It has come up the back road. While we look to the stars it overtakes the avenues. This is its method. The canals are almost captured and the boulevards are collapsing like bad veins. We have read the Bible and thought we would get off easy. It's too late to run, Gideon realized. He listened for the silken pressure just before a breaking wave, wanting to simply be with his mother.

This quiet desire, to be home, to be someone's son again, propelled the rest of his trip. As he pulled onto the gravel driveway of the former dairy, Gideon focused on the changes his mother had made, surprised at how much she forced out of the old, hoof-packed ground. Thick, controlled stands of bird of paradise led up from the mailbox like purple and orange flocks at the edge of a river. The bougainvillea, pruned from its former mounded sprawl, now trellised over the broadest side of the house so that its greenish white bracts looked like pods of ripening fruit. She had brought the lawn back all the way to the drive and he imagined her coaxing it with weekly increments of water.

The sky was a heavy blue, a ceramic shade which made the house look freshly painted white. Pansies and California poppies grew all around in tin saucepans and old pressure cookers. "You going to gawk all day?" his mother said from an upstairs window. "Put some work clothes on and meet me out back." Her voice was to him light and direct, like falling ash. How could he tell this woman he was sick, he wondered. He blocked the sun from his eyes to locate her, but only saw the empty space where she had been. All the windows on the second floor were original; wavy-looking, even from the outside. His mother liked the effect and he was not surprised there were still no screens.

Knowing she would not come out front, he went to his old room to change into jeans and a Dodgers T-shirt. Gideon stood still, looking at the new wallpaper—lime green with lateral rows of purple specks, visible up close as African violets. His mother had replaced his single bed with a queen size, covered by a white chenille spread hanging to the floor. He opened the closet and looked directly to the center of the empty hanger pole. His deeply scratched initials stained with black ink were preserved, everything around them recently painted.

Gideon threw his bags on the bed and lay back.

He listened for the sounds a house makes when it seems there are no sounds at all. When he was young, his mother told him there were people who lived in the walls and the creaks he heard were their tiny doors opening and closing. Over a period of time, his mother named these little beings, gave them each a story, and told him how they visited with her at midnight. Now, as he stared up at the old ceiling, a broad, private smile came over his face. He remembered the room cast in a dark, cloistered blue and the times he left his closet door cracked open, pretending to sleep in order to catch a miniature person walking across the floor. Sometimes he convinced himself he could see a head peeking around the bottom edge. In the morning he would tell his mother and it would be a secret between them.

Now he heard a pop of the old wood and he got up from the bed. Despite the changes, it was still his room.

After he put on his yard clothes, Gideon located his mother in back of the house pulling chaparral stumps from the ground. She breathed through a red bandanna tied at the back of her head. The dust and pollen she stirred were primary to him, like the peppery smell before a thunderstorm. He walked to his mother, twigs crushing beneath his feet. "Anna Jo Cavanaugh, your son is here," he said.

"Gideon James Cavanaugh, grab a pick." She turned around and slipped off the bandanna revealing the distinct swath of dirt on her upper face. Standing next to his mother, he felt the perspective of looking up even though he was eight inches taller than she. She was still beautiful to him; something produced by the West, he thought, rugged and exotic like manzanita in September. She hugged him, leaving her gloves on. "How's television production?" she continued. "Still brainwashing?"

"You taught me well."

Anna smiled quickly and pulled her son by the arm to the

cleared area to mark out where the roasting pits would be. They startled a covey of quail out of the brush, the birds flying just over their heads, a dozen brown spades disappearing into the sage on the upper hillside.

"This is where we had the fire walk," Gideon said, remembering the scarred ground left by a bed of oak cinders. When he was eleven his mother hosted a self-confidence seminar culminating in a walk across fifteen feet of hot coals. The cinderous gash in the lawn was the only source of light other than two red paper lanterns moving in the night like hot cigarette tips. The guests sat listening to the speaker who wore a black jump suit, making his head look detached from his body in the dim glow. Gideon detected a pattern early—the repeated words "conquer" and "overcome" and "visualize."

After three hours, the guests moved to the edge of the fire bed. One by one they stepped across the coals like they were charging a door. The objective was to focus on the end, concentrate on the wetted grass and feel nothing during the dash over the coals. Gideon watched the participants' faces as they finished their crossings. No one smiled or spoke. A woman squinted and checked her feet for blisters. She came and sat close to Gideon, watching the rest of the group go through the process. Their faces were cast in a hot, bleached orange. "What did it feel like?" Gideon asked the woman.

She was quiet for a moment, running her nails across the dark bottoms of her feet. "I don't remember how it felt."

Even years later, Gideon could pick out the bare spot in the ground where the coals had been and where he sat with the woman on the grass. "We're going to cook three lambs and a pig," Anna continued, breaking Gideon out of thought. "I'm expecting about two hundred, everybody that's even slightly related. You're the only one I wasn't sure would make it. Your track record isn't so great."

"I told you I was coming," Gideon said. But there was no heart in his reply. He thought of all the times he had been invited home but canceled at the last minute. His family had been the casualty of his success and he knew it. He had given them up for evenings watching friends sing at the CineGrill, or going dancing at warehouse clubs which changed locations every weekend. But most often, Gideon was simply immersed in production, and looking back, he realized his family was the first part of him he let go.

"You're here now," Gideon's mother said. "I guess I better put you to work." She smiled and pulled the bandanna over her mouth again. Gideon quickly surveyed the area she had already cleared. It was not large enough and he was glad he was there to help her. They began removing the remaining dandelion and wild mustard, working together on a larger perimeter.

The night of the reunion, when most of the relatives had gone, a few remained in the anesthesia of the warm evening. They sat in the bourbon-tinted light of the living room, finishing dishes of vanilla ice cream as the chime of spoons on glass gave way to the sound of crickets and air seasoned by pomegranate and trampled grass.

Gideon tried not to look tired and wondered if anyone noticed. It made him nervous, allowing for a clarity of thought he had given up in Los Angeles.

"I can't believe we did it," his mother said, putting her hands behind her head. "One hundred-and-eighty-three people and not one argument. That's a record on both counts for this family."

But Gideon was not listening. He sat at the edge of the room near the windows, aware of his own breathing, of his chest rising and falling, keeping time to the quiet pace of night. He wondered whether he had missed some change in himself which was only obvious to those who hadn't seen him in a long time.

Anna hit Gideon in the head with a pillow. "What's the matter with you? I was gloating. Fall in line."

"You were amazing," Gideon said, lobbing the pillow back. "I can't believe you got everyone to come." He looked at the few family members sitting around the room. His Great-uncle Ed slept, leaning on Gideon's grandmother. Ed junior sat across from his father, looking like a "before" picture, black hair and wide shoulders, always wearing an optimistic smile. Gideon felt he should have said more but he had no words, and the small group turned to his grandmother as she began to straighten out the lineages of people who had been there that day, doubling back on herself to correct links, then lingering over certain details. Gideon watched his family and thought about the black-and-white photograph at home of his Aunt Helen as a young girl. His mother had sent it to him. Except for her, he had rarely heard anyone speak of his aunt.

"Your grandparents had a farmhouse just like this in Missouri," Gideon's grandmother said to his mother. "By now they would've been in bed two hours already.

"It's funny how you forget about time. When I was a little girl

I clocked the day by how the sun hit my body." She stopped for a moment, raking Great-uncle Ed's white hair as he continued to sleep, then turned to Gideon's mother.

"Your father and I would sit straight through the summer on the wood porch, in earshot of our parents, of course. If it was late, twilight divided the barnyard into purple and black. He'd hold my hand and tell me what they had planted. All they tried to do all day was keep the insects away and the ground wet. He told me he fell asleep at night imagining the crickets were saying my name. He was a good man."

"What about Aunt Helen?" Gideon asked, the words leaving his mouth as quickly as he thought them.

The family sat for a moment, still and uncomfortable in the ticking surge of yellow light. Anna got up and nervously gathered their ice-cream dishes, taking them into the summer kitchen. The door flapped dull in its frame. Years of paint left tiny enamel stalactites hanging from the hinges.

"We don't talk about that," Gideon's grandmother said, nudging Great-uncle Ed off her shoulder.

But Gideon had not wanted to talk about Helen either. It had just come out, perhaps a simple claim of space for his aunt, the girl in the picture with two long braids and a plaid dress. Now, Gideon listened for sounds from the kitchen, for the clap of a closing cupboard or drawer. There was nothing. Outside, the breeze changed direction over the roasting pits, sending the smell of their insulation into the house, tin roofing, burlap and palm fronds—the mixture buttery and toxic like a serum for fever.

Gideon knew of his aunt only from the fragments of

information he had collected over the years, brief unintended disclosures prompted by family parties and quilted photo albums. Helen was fourteen years older than his mother. On her eighteenth birthday she announced she was going to be married to a man whose name changed in the family stories. Sometimes it was Chavez, other times Rodriguez. There was not much more reliable in Gideon's memory. The rest was his deduction that she was also pregnant and that his grandfather disowned her.

"I thought I could get through this," Anna said. "Today was going to be a new starting point. Family is the one thing in life we should count on."

"I shouldn't have brought it up," Gideon said.

"Somebody should have years ago. Of all people, family members should be honest with each other."

Gideon leaned back in his chair. He looked for words. The kitchen was ventilated on three sides by open windows lined with Depression glassware. In the only closed window, a slip of ivy had invaded an old bullet hole in the pane. The vine wound in and out of the creamers, tea cups, and saucers which tossed pastel clumps of pink and green light on the wood floor. Originally, the room had been used for cooking in the summer but Gideon remembered his mother rarely used the other kitchen. She liked it here because no matter what she was cooking, it smelled of the yard.

"This is a starting point," Gideon began. "You have to know something about me."

Anna got up and went to the cupboard, pulling down two cans of cat food, then cranking them on an opener bolted to the wall. "I'm your mother. Don't you think I already know? I understand the difference between best friend and boyfriend." Anna took the opened containers and set them on the stairs outside. She stood watching out the screen door. "The possums will be up shortly."

"Why didn't you say something?"

"Because I wonder. For your sake, do you want to bring that into this family? When I left that room, you were the only one who came after me. They can turn things off so easily. I don't want my son forgotten."

Gideon stood up and walked to his mother, feeling armed. He heard the cat food already being dragged down the steps. They might have more than one reason to forget, he thought to himself. The dark was warm and uncomfortably familiar. Gideon shook because he had been to this precipice before. It had ended his last relationship. We mark time by the calm of night, he thought. It is a coalescence of disclosure, words filtered over candles or bridged between pillows. "Mom, I'm sick," he said.

Anna looked outside, squinting her eyes to catch the tiny bodies carrying the cans away. "Yes. I thought so," she said, finally, quietly.

She pulled the pencil from her hair, something she did when she was most relaxed. Gideon remembered this was how she appeared when she read to him at night when he was a boy, her black hair stricken white by reflection. She reached out from her side without turning to him. "Is this between us, Gideon?" She allowed her son to consider the history of the people who had come to the reunion that day, knowing he would not want to become a family myth. "You can come home," his mother said.

"I'm no better than them, Mom. I've pushed my family to the back of my life." Gideon took a deep breath and managed a smile, hoping his mother understood this was not another act of separation. "Besides, this seems scary now, but someday I'll just be an old-fashioned AIDS story."

Anna took her son's hands in hers. "I guess it's too late to live any other way for both of us," she said. "And would we really want to?"

It is this night Gideon thinks of as he sits on his deck, waiting for his mother to arrive from San Diego. A pair of jets make vapor-trail sutures across the sky, the scars healing from their farthest point. He knows it is five o'clock by the specific gradation of yellow. It is the easiest time for him to breathe, looking at the back-lit olive trees and Spanish-style homes, the increasing sound of traffic washing insinuation from the air. He realizes he is waiting for that transition which never comes to Los Angeles: people, like certain perennials, coaxed into extended seasons. He examines his hands, convinced he can feel the skin pulling back from his nails. They are dry and peeling in minute strands.

Gideon looks at the adjacent hill a mile off, everything behind it a vague, petroleum orange. At the top of the hill stands a single palm, a black and accidental keyhole after the sunset. He drove to it once. The tree's base was covered with nails and staples from years of lost dogs and yard sales. It seemed unaffected, it's rustling crown of fronds thick and new, making the air sound carbonated. But now its form is simply dark and distant.

Looking out at Los Angeles from his home, he begins to understand the geometry of lights, a plain of red dust and halogen shards. It is like a bed of hot coals he has just crossed. A quarter moon sits low in the sky, tinted orange like a dim lantern. The light falls on Gideon's skin like dying flame. He feels the oncoming night and people like himself making decisions that will change their lives. We are consumed like fuel, he thinks, and we are cautious because every twilight is a fire walk.

He considers the intricate processes of preparation and how he will be remembered. They will say he was successful. He had a career and a house with a view. But it has all come down to reversion, as if he has recreated an expectant mother waiting for his birth. I have relinquished myself, Gideon thinks. He had counted on his life's momentum and now it is leaving him as he sits alone on the deck of his backyard. He accepts the conditions of this final inertia, the feeling he is slipping, falling back, and he hopes his mother will arrive in time to catch him.

Who Knew Her Best

————||||||||————

You don't meet too many people like us every day. It's not like we go around saying what we do, and when we do it, it's usually pretty private. I guess that makes it sound kind of mysterious, which is not what I mean to do at all. I'm just a screenwriter. Not one of those big-budget Hollywood types, but I do okay. Had a couple things at Sundance. One in Toronto. Got something now in post-production. I specialize in character studies, I guess, real intimate stuff where plot is secondary to understanding the characters. This is what people say I'm good at, so I do it. They say *I know people*. But to be honest, I'm not so sure. I try. I use bits and pieces from people I meet to make one "real" character. But to really know a person, well, I don't know if that's possible, which I suppose is why I can't seem to get this down as a screenplay. Because it can't be all chopped up and reassembled in some marketable symmetry.

(May. Burbank Airport. A single-story length of building painted institutional beige. The sky is a dull blue, but clear. There are three small clouds in the sky. The air is heavy with the sound of jet engines idling, landing, and taking off. Interior of a late-model Lexus.)

It was my first day on the job, but Zen Lee was easy to spot. She stood at the curb, all four-foot-ten of her, a hyper-blonde draped in a long dark green raincoat that made her look pregnant. Behind her were Daniel, a gophery-looking bodyguard, and Janice, her hair and makeup artist.

Zen slid into the front seat and I popped the trunk while the other two loaded their luggage. "You're new, so I'll cut you a break," she said. "Next time meet us at the gate or I'll tell Larry to get another driver." Larry was Zen's agent and manager and my new boss. I'd met him at a party and mentioned I was having trouble finding work, not just any work, but industry work. I'd just moved from Michigan and wasn't too smooth on knowing how to get in. Larry said he had a car and needed a driver for some of his clients while he showed my first screenplay around. He told me that I'd mainly be responsible for Zen, that she was his ticket and I should treat her well no matter what.

So, I just smiled at Zen. "Next time the gate," I said.

"Right." She gave a sharp nod. I'd never seen any of her films, but she didn't look like what I imagined an actress looked like, especially for her kind of movies. She wore no makeup, and except for the dark eyes, her Chinese features were pale and flat. She slipped off her coat, revealing what I learned was her trademark, an elfin body and outsized breasts, the kind women on pinball machines have. The kind that were practically the whole reason I bought comic books when I was twelve.

The other two got into the back seats. Everyone was conspicuously quiet. I'd never met them before and they didn't ask my name. "James," I said. "My name is James." I looked in the rearview mirror. Daniel and Janice mumbled.

As I pulled away, Zen opened her purse and produced a pack of menthols. Instead of cigarettes, she pulled out a wad of money-clipped cash. Daniel and Janice slid up close, Janice breathing in my right ear. They were like two anxious children. Zen handed them each a few bills. "Here's to a rotten fucking weekend." She watched as they counted their shares.

"Not what I figured," Daniel said and Janice agreed.

"Who paid the bar tab? And all that blow didn't go up *my* nose." Zen turned to me in explanation. "Coke."

"That's fair," Janice said. "We had to do something though. They so didn't like us." Her voice was high and wheezy, like a squeeze toy.

Daniel sat back, tucking his money into his shirt pocket. "They're pricks alright. *China Doll* was a great flick. And *Jungle Girls*."

Zen turned around in her seat, facing them both. "It's all politics. Four nominations and not one award? Think about some of the pigs they make me work with—like that Frank guy. Politics." She slouched into the seat. "I don't want to hear another word about it."

"It's a good thing you didn't have your gun," Janice said.

Larry hadn't told me where they had been. He just asked if I'd ever seen one of Zen's movies and when I said I hadn't, he showed me a picture of her. It was a color still of Zen on her back. Her hair lay perfectly over her shoulders, shiny purple lips exaggerated, apart in that expression that's somewhere between pain and pleasure, and her long-lashed eyes passively closed. "Where were you guys?" I asked as we left the airport.

"Adult Film Awards," Janice said, almost simultaneously to Daniel's "Las Vegas."

Zen slapped her small thigh, her long red fingernails grating the fabric of her tight slacks. "I'm the best thing out there right now and next year I'll be even bigger."

"Icarus, babe," Daniel said in a cautionary voice. "Icarus."

"Will you knock it off with that Icarus crap." Zen buckled herself in as we got onto the freeway. "I bet you don't even know who Icarus is."

"He's the dude with the plastic wings that flew too close to the sun."

I looked in the mirror, watching Daniel's satisfied smile. Up close, he was more beavery than gophery. "Wax," I finally said. "I'm pretty sure his wings were wax."

Zen gave me a brief smile and winked.

"Right. That's right," Janice added. "They didn't have plastic back then."

Daniel wasn't happy. He ran his fingers through his prematurely gray hair. "Let's just get home."

I nodded. Daniel and Janice closed their eyes and leaned their heads against the windows and Zen fished a pair of sunglasses out of her purse, slipped them on, and reclined in her seat. And the three of them shut down as if they were toys who'd just been switched off.

It wasn't such a bad job. I was used to driving my father's meat truck around Ypsilanti. That's what I did before I wrote screenplays. I drove a truck selling meat door-to-door. It took me a long time, but after twelve years in my father's business, I packed two suitcases worth of clothes, kissed my girlfriend, Gainy, goodbye, and headed out to Hollywood. My father'd shown me lots of things about meat-cutting, of course. But more importantly, he taught me how to *sell* meat. If Mrs. Brewster didn't want brisket on Friday, if we didn't sell it all day, we could go to Mr. Jacks in the afternoon and tell him we saved a special cut and he'd buy it. We could do that with just about anyone, except Mrs. Handel, who was Rolled Rump, Rolled Rump, Rolled Rump and nothing else. And you have to have a recipe, always a new recipe, in case a customer looks bored or is afraid to try something, especially something you've got too much of or that another customer decides against. Something like the one for Pickled Beef Heart. *Cook as you would a Smoked Beef Tongue. Add ⅔ cup vinegar to stock when heart is tender. Allow heart to remain in stock several hours. Drain and chill. Slice and serve with piquant sauce.*

From that to driving around people like Zen. It wasn't much different, I decided. Most of Larry's clients were pretty cool. No one big. But the fact they had someone driving them around made them feel successful. It's pretty unusual for an agent/manager to send a car out for people whose whole careers are built on cereal and toothpaste commercials. But Larry had a lot of clients and he said this was an investment, a small kindness that would pay off if any of them hit it big. Zen was his best shot. Maybe a whole new direction in his management since she was his only client in porn.

(June. Hollywood Hills, Griffith Park Observatory. The bright sun refracts off a haze covering Hollywood below.)

Sometimes Zen didn't want me to take her right to a shoot. We'd make some side trip so she could get an ice cream or a pop. I always stayed in the car and waited for her. But as we parked at the observatory she turned to me, her hair twisted up in some approximation of a bun. "My treat," she said, almost giggling. So we got some pop at the concession stand and started walking around, not talking at first.

The observatory is this old 1920s thing, built out in the country at the time, but now pinched between Hollywood and the sprawl of the San Fernando Valley. It's like an art deco wart rising out of the chaparral-covered hills. They've shot some movies there, like *Rebel Without a Cause*. There's even a gaunt, dark-eyed statue of James Dean.

"He was lucky," Zen said, running her hand along the base.

"What do you mean?" I said. "He died before he got to be somebody."

Zen sipped from her pop, darkening the purple lipstick ring on her straw. "He died *just* as he got to be somebody. Perfect."

"I don't get it," I said. My pop was almost gone.

"No. You wouldn't," Zen said.

I shook the ice around in my cup and went for a three-pointer in a distant trashcan. It bounced off the side, the ice spraying out onto the concrete. "All I know is if I were famous, I'd want to stay on top. And that means staying alive." I walked to the trashcan and picked up my cup to throw it away.

Zen laughed. "You're a good boy. Aren't you?"

I didn't know what to say to that. We walked to the edge overlooking Hollywood with its windows and cars and heat all glimmering from beneath the haze. The dusty smell of sage and sumac tickled past us. "So what's your deal, Farm Boy?" Zen asked. "I mean... what's your deal?"

"Thanks for the clarification." I laughed and looked at her. She'd taken her hair out of its bun and the light breeze flicked it around her face. For the first time I thought she was pretty. "To start with, just because I like plaid shirts doesn't make me a farm boy. I'm more like a suburb boy. Other than that, I'm just out here to sell my screenplay."

"No girlfriend?"

"Yeah, her name is Gainy."

Zen paused and nodded. "Of course," she said quietly, "of course."

"We've been going out a while now." I hadn't really talked to anyone about Gainy since I moved. The hairs of my forearm refracted gold under the sun and I nervously ran my fingers over their softness. I realized, too, that I was tired of Zen thinking of me as a farm boy. "Gainy's Black," I blurted.

Zen laughed. "Babe," she said, "that don't get you any points in L.A. We do that every day here." She wrapped her hair back into its bun and started humming something I didn't recognize, something random and childlike. When her hair was fixed, she looked directly at me and tapped one of her long white nails on my chin. "And besides, is that really the first thing you have to say about your girlfriend?"

"No," I stumbled, "I...she...it's more than that. You don't know me so I thought I'd tell you something interesting."

"That's the point. You see, I don't think that *is* really interesting. I've had a lot of guys in my movies, white, black, whatever. Their dicks all feel the same."

"I guess I wanted you to know I wasn't some provincial hick."

"We'll get to know each other after a while. After a few drinks, maybe. You're not a lost cause. But shit like that isn't going to get you anywhere. If you want to know people, you can't work from the outside." Zen spun around and started walking back toward the car.

I jogged up next to her. "Don't get me wrong. I have a pretty keen sense about people."

She continued walking without looking at me, but smiling. "Trust me. You won't really know that about yourself until you find someone who's deep in it—I mean, neck-deep—and you realize you're the only one who knows how to pull them out."

(*July. Top-level parking garage, Los Angeles International Airport. It's hot, nearly one hundred degrees. Everything is heat-glazed. The sky is white with sun.*)

Janice wasn't with them on that trip. It was just Zen and Daniel. And me carrying half their luggage across the lot. "I don't think I'm getting paid for this," I said.

"Icarus," Daniel said. "Wax wings and all that shit."

I looked at Zen but she just laughed. "I don't care how much it costs me," she said to Daniel. "My hair looked like hell the whole time."

They were returning from Hawaii. The real money for Zen, I began to understand, was not in making movies, but in her personal appearances at strip joints. In major cities, she could pull down a few thousand dollars for three nights.

"Jesus, it's hot," she said as we approached the car. "Feels like the sun is ten feet away." She was wearing the green raincoat as usual, but I knew she wouldn't take it off until we got in the car.

"Maybe L.A. is Icarus," Daniel said.

"Are you still high?" Zen plopped her bags near the car trunk. "Enough with the Icarus. Read another book."

Up to then, I was pretty quiet. I'd learned to gauge their moods on these return trips. They were fine when I dropped them off, but by the time they came back, sometimes they could be pretty harsh. We loaded the bags in the trunk and, as soon as we were all in the car, I flipped on the air-conditioning. "So it was a good trip?" I asked. Not because of anything they said, but because for the first time they didn't still smell completely of cigarettes, and their eyes were fairly clear.

"Five thou," Zen said.

Daniel leaned forward. "Speaking of which."

She counted out his pay. "You gotta keep those creeps from touching me. That's what you're for."

"You don't know half the trouble I keep you out of."

Zen looked at me and told me about how during one of her

sets done to a disco version of David Bowie's "China Girl," she snapped off her top and a few guys ran up to the stage with wads of bills. Except one young guy reached out and grabbed her breasts. "And you have to keep dancing," she said to me, "or the whole set is ruined and you lose all that money."

Daniel cut in. "Their bouncers should've been there."

Zen shook her head and I realized I could hear the dryness and strawlike rasp of her bleached hair. "Next time I'll talk to them. I keep a gun at home. But *you're* my gun on the road. And maybe you should lay off the coke."

"*Me?*" Daniel said. "You're fried three days straight and I do a couple lines and *I* need to lay off?"

"Look at all the bullshit I go through. You'd be high, too."

By then we were on the 405 headed toward the 10 and back to Hollywood. I'm still not quite sure where one city ends and another begins. It's all Los Angeles to me. And it was hot. Not Michigan hot, like when it's ninety-five outside and humid. The hot in L.A. is different. It tears at your skin. It's dry. LAX is on the coast, but after you get just a few miles inland, you'd never know the Pacific was anywhere near. "It's been like this ever since you two left," I said.

"It's July," Daniel said.

Zen sighed. "That's the thing I miss about Washington. It gets hot but it doesn't last."

I'd never heard her talk about living anywhere other than Los Angeles. "How'd you end up here."

"School didn't work out. Asshole father. Long story."

Daniel sat forward in his seat and looked at me in the rearview mirror. He'd cut his hair down to crew length and it made his eyes look bluer and wider than usual. "Listen to experience," he said. "I know Zen better than anyone. Change the topic."

Zen had a serious look on her face. "I'll tell you that crap later on when I'm less tired and more drunk," she said.

"What about you?" Daniel asked. "What are you doing out here. Besides that script crap, I mean." He started to laugh and Zen joined in. "Sorry, man," he continued. "It's just that every joker and his mother comes out here with a script."

For a moment, I said nothing. Why defend myself to a bratty porn actress and her half-wit bodyguard? I saw downtown Los Angeles in the hazy distance. We were in the third lane, the best place to drive if you have the nerve for last-second lane changes to make your exit. "I'll tell you what I'm doing out here," I started out. "Not that you'll understand." I explained how I worked my way through college in my dad's meat business. How I got my degree in English, that piece of paper that pleased my mother so much, my mother the librarian who I visited at work almost every day nearly through high school. Sometimes I helped her shelve books. Sometimes I read. And when I got older, sometimes after work we'd go see a film because she wrote reviews for the local paper. That's where I learned to appreciate movies, those early evenings when Mom and I walked outside after a film and started talking about it. We almost always agreed, though my mother developed an inexplicable one-sided feud with Steven Spielberg. "Somehow," I said, "between that and Dad's business, I think I've figured out people pretty well. Most of all, I realized this script I've fiddled with for five years was just going to sit on my desk if

I didn't do something. I'd be married and selling meat and I'd never know."

When I finished, I looked directly at Zen. "The dream thing," she said.

"I guess."

Daniel sat back, "Think you got people figured out, Farm Boy?"

"Pretty much," I said. And I meant that. It never took me long to see what makes a person tick. I was sure I could practically read Gainy's mind. My Mom and Dad's, too. Anyone I knew long enough.

(Late August. On Interstate 5 headed toward the San Fernando Valley. Santa Ana winds have blown all the haze and pollution over the Pacific. The valley is a carpet of tract homes, strip malls, and asphalt intersections. Interior of a late-model Lexus.)

"It's really nice of you to take me out to the shoot," Janice said.

"Larry says not to make a habit of it." I liked Janice okay, but she was a little clingy and there was always something odd about the way she looked. Her skin kind of hung on her bones as if she lost a lot of weight in a hurry, or maybe she was going to be fat in old age and her skin was thinking ahead. I don't know. And for a hair and makeup artist, someone Zen swore by, Janice's hair was always matty and flat in all the wrong places, like she'd used too much relaxer. But maybe it was fashionable and I just didn't get it. And her clothes consisted almost entirely of jeans and wrinkly oversized men's shirts.

"Larry won't do anything. Zen asked for me," she said. "We're pretty tight." She looked at me and I nodded. "Like sisters. Really."

"I'm sure," I said, but what I wanted to say was *everyone* said that about Zen. Even Larry had said he knew Zen like she was his own daughter, only he didn't have a daughter, or any children for that matter. Just an annoying iguana, Carmine, that sat on the floor of his office under a heat lamp.

"You know what?" Janice said.

I waited.

"Zen isn't Zen. Her name is Susan."

"Interesting." I'd never thought about Zen having another name. Maybe because I'd still not bothered to rent one of her movies, though Daniel kept offering to loan me one of his.

"Right. Right. Susan Cheung, daughter of a chicken farmer. Home town, Blue Falls, Washington. She doesn't talk to her family though."

"You sound like a press release."

"She's my only client now. I know her backward and forward." Janice stopped herself and sat back in her seat. "Of course, all that stuff is confidential."

"Between you and me," I said.

"Right. She'd totally kill me."

I thought for a moment. Janice was smiling, a bit triumphant that she'd validated her connection to Zen. "But how can she be your only client?"

"Why not?"

"Seems risky," I said. "If something happens to her, what happens to you?"

"I'm not worried. I've had the big jobs." She made quotation signs with her fingers around big jobs. "But those people are assholes. They just want to use you, the slicks and the studios. With Zen, she's a guaranteed star and I'm in on the ground level. And it's all under the table with a little bazooka on the side." She stopped and read the question on my face. "I forgot who I was talking to. Bazooka is cocaine." I thought she was done, but she added one more thing and it sounded rehearsed or like she'd heard someone else say it. "You gotta ride the wave when it comes."

"I guess," I said. "But every wave slams into the shore, Janice."

"Right. Right." She smiled and wet her fingers, patting down a bit of hair, as if it could make a difference, and I could tell she didn't understand what I was saying.

I never know for sure, but I think it was that moment when I thought I had these people pegged. Their work is about screwing, I thought, and their friendships are about screwing and sometimes they accidentally get sober enough to almost understand that and they send someone out for more drugs before anything gets too real.

Then there was me every night in my Echo Park studio apartment, barely enough room to take a full breath, sitting in front of the TV, eating spaghetti or whatever macaroni and cheese was on sale, just hoping that the next day someone would pick up *Orchard* and say "This is a great fucking script," and then Larry would beep me and I'd get a check and go home, no, I'd bring home to *me*. Bring Gainy and my mom and dad all out to California for a visit. That was my plan and I thought about it every night during every commercial and every night I fell asleep to either that thought or Ricky and Fred bailing Lucy and Ethel out of another black-and-white predicament. In the morning, I'd wake up, the television still on and the first human voices of the day talking about movie grosses or TV ratings.

(December. Late evening. Hollywood Boulevard and Gardner, a residential mix of art deco homes and apartments. Above are the Hollywood Hills dotted with lights giving over to the dark silhouettes of hilltops.)

As always, I walked Zen to the door. It had been a late shoot and she looked tired. Not just physically tired, but a kind of deflated tired. She stood one step higher than me as we said goodnight. "I like it when you bring me home," she said. "It always feels like a first date."

I didn't know what to say. Normally I would have gone home right then, but Zen sat on the steps and patted the spot next to her, so I sat down, too. Driving her to and from the shoot that day was the first time I'd seen her since before Thanksgiving and she seemed different. Maybe Zen was being nicer because I didn't fight back, maybe because I wasn't worth it. Whatever the reason, she wasn't being so combative.

Zen lit a cigarette and stared across the street. "Can you believe I live right next to a church?"

I squinted and barely made out the name of the small stone structure. "Episcopalian," I said. "It doesn't count."

Zen laughed and tapped the ash off her cigarette, the remaining cinder a tiny orange heart floating in the air. We were quiet for a moment and then she looked at me. "My name is really Susan," she said.

"Janice told me something about that."

"Of course she did. Janice couldn't keep her mouth shut for anything."

"So I guess the chicken ranch stuff is true?"

"Eggs," Zen said. "It's an egg ranch." She put out her half-smoked cigarette and turned her body toward me, bringing her knees up to her chest. "Or *was*. I don't really know if my father's still working. I don't talk to him."

I leaned back on the stairs, cautious. "Why's that?"

Zen looked at the street. "There's a pomegranate tree in front of that apartment building. Last year Daniel and I picked tons of them. That's what's so cool about L.A. Every tree in the world grows here." She started pointing. "All the palms. And the jacaranda, those are my favorite. I didn't even know what they were until I came here. My neighbor says they're Brazilian but they seem like they belong. I guess they're stuck here like the rest of us." She paused for a moment and turned back to me. "Two reasons why I don't talk to my father. He didn't get ahold of me when my mother died." She stopped again, tucking her hair behind her ears and then with a very serious tone she said, "And I guess I don't want to explain to him what I'm doing. They sent me down here for school."

I didn't know what to say, so I nodded.

"It's like, I know you wanted me to be an engineer, Daddy, but I'm doing porn now."

"That would be a shock," I said.

"It's more than that. It's a Chinese thing. A debt owed to parents. Honorable repayment and crap like that. But I've changed way too much for him to handle. I mean, I left school because I realized I couldn't live up to my parents' expectations. I wanted to do something else. Interior Design, or act. And I met Larry and he got me a couple parts. But there aren't too many roles for Asians and then Larry asked me if I wanted to do a nude pool scene in a movie, just stand around. The money was good."

What was I thinking then as Zen told me more about herself than everything she'd ever said to me combined? I remember the blue Christmas lights in the window of an apartment across the street and the sound of the breeze running through the palms along the boulevard, a relentless sweeping noise. And it seems now I should've asked Zen different questions. But honestly, I don't think my mind was on that moment. I hadn't heard a single positive thing about my screenplay and I was considering going back to Michigan where I had life pretty well figured. "So that was the start," I said. "The pool scene."

"I guess. I really did just stand around. But the director talked to Larry about me." She pointed at her breasts. "And they paid for my first set of these. It seems pretty abrupt when I talk about it, but L.A. changes everyone."

"So what has it done to me?"

Zen smiled softly. "You've got a tan now, that's one good thing." She broke off. "I don't know you that well. I guess I figure you for the type of guy who'll marry a blonde wife and your wedding night will be your first time and then you'll have 2.5 blonde, freckly kids. But all I *really* know is that you've got the script. What's going on with that?"

I shrugged. "Larry says he's still showing it around."

"Let me stop you right there. Maybe one of us should've said this earlier. Get an agent. Because if you aren't making money for Larry, he's not doing anything for you."

I started to break in, but Zen stopped me.

"I don't care what he says. Trust me, he's not doing you any favors."

"I was starting to wonder," I said. "Like maybe I should change the name to *Fatal Orchard* or *Orchard Impact*." Zen laughed. "Sometimes," I said, "I think I should just go back to delivering meat. I liked it. Just marry Gainy and have kids, though I doubt they'll be blonde and freckly."

Zen looked surprised. "You're engaged?"

"Not yet."

She squinted, an unasked question on her face.

"But we will be," I said.

"So you've talked about it?"

"Not really."

Zen leaned over and patted me on the shoulder. "Sometimes I wonder about you. You're a bit older than me, but you don't know people very well. You better talk to her. Especially with this long distance thing. At least I *know* I don't have my shit together." After she said that, she kind of receded. You could see it in the way she pulled back and turned around so that she was facing the street again.

"I guess we could both use some work," I said. "And for the record, I had sex when I was thirteen. My mom found out and she brought home a book from the library on childrearing and made my dad read me the facts of life."

"At least your dad talked to you about it," Zen said. "I had to learn from one really awful date."

I looked at her and she shook her head as if I shouldn't ask. "But it's what we do *now* that counts. I just uprooted myself and came here. It isn't as easy as I hoped, but I'm here. You could take some classes, some Interior Design. It's not too late."

"Yeah, I could do that," she said. "Maybe something over at LACC. They've got all kinds of stuff there. Maybe I'll check it out Monday."

"Movies don't have to be your life. I mean, you could go back to school and maybe even call your dad."

She half-smiled as she stood up. "I could."

We said goodnight again and Zen gave me a brief hug, the first in all the time we'd known each other. She went inside and I felt good at that moment. As if we'd gotten through to each other. As if maybe she'd call Larry on Monday and tell him she wasn't doing porn anymore. In my mind, she was already enrolled in school.

As I walked back to my car, past Zen's living room window, I heard a crash, the sound of glass breaking. There was a thin, scrimlike curtain but I could see inside. Everything was white, the furniture, the walls. And Zen was facing away from me, bent down, picking up glass off the wood floor. A purple iris lay next to her, so I guessed it was a vase she'd broken. For a moment, I thought to go to the door to see if she was okay. But it was just a vase and we ended on such a good moment, I thought. I didn't want to ruin it. I'd see her on Monday, maybe drive her to school instead of the shoot.

World Famous Love Acts

(Mid-December. Backyard of a North Hollywood home. There is an oval swimming pool and a small lawn with sixty white folding chairs, nearly all of them occupied. The left front row is empty except for a gray-haired Chinese man.)

I took a seat in the back row and was surprised how many people attended Zen's memorial service, especially since it was so close to Christmas. I was pleased mostly, I guess, because her father was there. I didn't talk to him that day, but it was me who'd gotten him to come. At least I think. There was only one Cheung in Blue Falls, Washington. The first time I called, I got a machine and hung up. When I called again, I left a message with details about the service. I gave him Larry's number because he was supposedly taking care of the arrangements, even though I made most of the calls, and at his request, itemized everything for tax purposes. He paid for everything. It was his home, this reception, his service.

"I probably knew Zen better than anyone here," Larry said in his eulogy. "She was a good girl, dedicated to her craft and proud of her career. She was always looking forward, concerned with quality. She wanted to raise the standards of our industry."

As he spoke, I tried to remember a time I'd seen Larry and Zen together. Nothing came to mind. The woman next to me leaned close to my ear. "He looks good," she said.

"I suppose," I whispered. He was wearing a dark gray suit, Armani he told people at the reception. New, just for this occasion.

When he was done with his remarks, Larry invited others to offer their remembrances of Zen. Janice was the first to speak. "I've known Zen practically longer than anyone," she began. "Even before she started doing movies." As she spoke, I looked at Zen's father, but I couldn't tell if he had a reaction. I wondered what he was thinking, if he even recognized the woman being eulogized. Hadn't anyone thought to call her Susan? "Zen and I were like sisters," Janice continued. "I remember how we used to go thrift shopping and she picked out the worst things and somehow they looked good on her. And she called me late at night and we talked about all kinds of things. Boy troubles mostly." Janice rolled her eyes for comic effect and people laughed. "But the thing I admired most about Zen is that she was dedicated to her career. Always out on the road with me and Daniel. I don't know what I'm going to do without her. We were building our careers together and now she's gone." And then Janice started crying and Larry stood up to help her away, but she waved him off. I couldn't help thinking it was a wonderful advertisement.

A couple people I'd never met spoke, someone called Charles and a woman named Delia. They both talked about working with Zen and about how professional she was and how much she'd taught them even though she was so young. People were nodding in agreement and I wondered if we were listening to the same thing.

And after them was Daniel. "I was Zen's best friend," he began, and I didn't hear anything else. He was speaking but I blocked it all out. It was clear that this was a contest to prove who knew her best and I was thinking about what I was going to say, how I'd point out these people didn't really know Zen. I'd say her name was Susan and she wanted to do Interior Design or be a real actress. I could even name her favorite tree, jacaranda. But then I stopped myself and Daniel was winding up, too. Because what could I say about Zen beyond that? I'd had that one night with her on the stairs. And when I left, I thought everything was okay, that we'd shared the same moment of clarity. I didn't know the last time I'd see her would be through her living-room window, through the curtains, in a white room I assume she decorated herself. I couldn't even see her face as she picked up glass from the broken vase, if it was a vase. At best, I'd seen her when she was alone and didn't know anyone was watching and even then it was brief, not even important enough, apparently, for me to knock on her door to make sure she was alright. She was in it deep—neck-deep—as she'd said to me once, and I didn't even recognize it. All my suggestions had been simple, the outside things.

So I just sat and listened to Daniel finish. I let the service end without saying a word. I didn't know these people well enough to scold them. I didn't know Zen. I started thinking of home, of my mom and dad and Gainy and her family. And I was a little scared because what if I didn't know them either? And, I thought, if I don't understand the people I care for most, what the hell am I doing away from them? What am I doing out here?

Desdemona's Ruins

———||||||———

L ook for me in the dirt," Desdemona likes to say. That's where she's always been most comfortable, in the pit of a dig, earth caked at the tip of her nose, packed into her cracked hands and under her nails. She understands every grain before she brushes it away, knows the variations in the geology, can read the stratum like a map. This layer represents a flood. This, a volcanic eruption. She knows the way uncovered bone smells like fresh caraway, how buried objects can disintegrate from the work of a too-eager archaeologist. She's seen it, clay pots and scraps of beaded leather crumbling in inexperienced hands. This is why they call her to consult on a dig, why they have for twenty years. Desdemona can say *stop*.

It is March when the letter from her sister arrives in Xi'an. Her assistant finds Desdemona examining some of the partially uncovered terra-cotta warriors. It is unusual for anyone but a Chinese to be allowed in the pit, but Desdemona gets her way. "Letter from your sister, Dez," the young man calls down to her, holding the envelope.

She's kneeling at the far end of a row of perfectly restored clay statues, warriors still posed for battle, their hands empty of the swords and bows ransacked a millennium ago. Desdemona and the curators are examining the yellow clay and exposed arms and torsos of the remaining unexcavated army. She stands straight up, clamping her hands on her strong hips. "In the van," she directs. "I'll read it later."

"The problem," the translator says, "is that the warriors are fully colored, but when we remove them, the pigment remains in the surrounding earth."

"I know all about it," Desdemona says. She offers a coffee-tinted smile, understanding the effect of her presence, the big American woman with the rust-colored hair and sun-scarred skin. "I've read about it extensively."

"They want to know what is your advice?"

Desdemona takes in the building erected over the site, big as a jet hanger—exposed steel beams, just enough light for the tourists gawking over the railings. She knows the technology to save these artifacts, but it's costly and the Chinese don't have it. The Italians have already told them this but they have called her because she is the last word. "My advice," she says, looking at her hosts. "Don't dig. Not for a while. Sometimes you have to leave things buried to save them." She will not say it twice. She knows they will listen.

On the way back to the hotel Desdemona keeps her eyes on the broad stretches of farmland. "There's more out there," she says to her assistant.

"Don't forget about this." He hands her the letter from her sister.

She holds it a moment, looking at the flap sealed with a salmon-shaped sticker. She considers the fact it has been almost nine years since Madeleine last wrote. It had been a good letter, telling her she should visit. That she was loved and forgiven. Desdemona replied she would come as soon as work slowed. But Calcutta had popped up, then Mexico City, the little jobs in between. Then Xi'an. Goddamn, she thinks to herself, there's enough work in China to bury me. The handwriting is shaky. It was addressed to the university in early February and it is already late March. She turns the envelope over to the side with the salmon sticker, adding legs and arms to it with her pen. She draws progressive versions, each more upright until the last is recognizably human. *Homofishus*, she writes at the side. *Evolution*. She opens the envelope and extracts the letter written on lined white paper, the edges still frilled from being torn out of a spiral note pad. There are just a few bare words.

> Dear Sister,
>   I'm getting old. You're getting old. I wish you'd come see me.
>
>   Madeleine

"Anything the matter, Dez?" her assistant asks.

Desdemona takes a deep breath. She is glad it's nothing serious, nothing crisislike. "My sister just misses me." Desdemona looks again out the window at the dry landscape. She feels tectonic. After Xi'an, she tells herself, maybe I can take a break. After Xi'an. The stripped fields flash by, the rows blinking at her, the moment receding like everything else, becoming part of a deep interior current, a conversation in her own voice she does not yet hear.

I

Even as a young girl I was trying to burn off my accent. Madeleine couldn't care less about the way she spoke, but me, I didn't want anyone writing me off, thinking I was some backwoods hick. Not that anyone in Blue Falls talked any better, but we weren't from Washington and you could hear the Missouri in us. Mom asking us to "fetch" her something. Or Dad telling us he "know'd" this thing or that. Small words and phrases that made me itch, just want to crawl out of my skin and be someone else. Certainly not the thick girl with the purple birthmark on her temple in the shape of Africa. But I was me. Stuck, I thought.

When I was about sixteen, Madeleine and I took one of our trips high up on the Blue Falls River. She liked to trout-fish, something I could never figure out. Sitting around, feet getting wet no matter how hard we tried to stay out of the water. Hours of it all spent on a few fish. But the truth is, we had a good time. I hunted around for arrowheads and interesting stones and Madeleine fished.

That day I brought along Mom's garden spade and a length of screen Dad didn't seem to be using. Like usual, we loaded our things in the old Ford truck Madeleine got for her eighteenth birthday. About the most unsafe vehicle I've ever sat in. Passenger floorboard was so rusted out, Dad had to put in a piece of wood to keep your foot from falling through.

We kissed Mom goodbye. "You girls get back before dark," she said, like always. "Bring home some big'uns, Madeleine." Then she looked at me. "And some real pretty rocks."

I most like to think of Mom the way she looked when Madeleine was backing us out of the driveway that morning. She stood on the porch waving. She was wearing one of her simple cotton dresses, that going-gray red hair pinned back, the totem-pole apron that made her head the topmost figure, a living akrolith. There was the comfort of knowing she'd be waiting for us on the porch when we came back. I knew she'd probably be reading from one of her books she'd been through a thousand times already. If it was too dark for her to read, we knew we were late.

We drove further that day than we'd ever been by ourselves. Dad had taken us a long way before, but somehow, this seemed riskier. "Why the new spot?" I asked Madeleine.

"Figure you need some fresh dirt to dig in," she said. Which was true, I'd just about dug up every likely place for arrowheads in our normal spots.

"Thanks," I said. Even though we couldn't know it then, that gesture would change my whole life. Probably more important than anything Mom or Dad ever did for me, and they tried hard.

Madeleine reminded me a lot of Dad when we went fishing

because she would wear one of his old shirts and some overalls. That, and she had a big voice like Dad's. It wasn't so loud as much as it came right at you and made you listen whether you were interested or not.

We found a place to park and took our gear into the woods, her with a tackle box and rod, me with our lunch, my screen and the spade. When you live up there, you take for granted what a good day is like, but if I had to pick one out, that would be as good as any. It was summer and there wasn't a cloud in the sky but it wasn't too hot either, and the air smelled sweet as the just-out-of-the-shell walnuts we helped Mom with around the holidays.

We had to press our way through the underbrush, usually, knowing Mom would be shaking her head at all the scratches on our faces. But that day, the forest floor seemed to open up for us. There's something remarkable about walking through the woods, the canopy sifting the breeze so it sounds like water, and then you come to that intangible line, when the sound of the river sneaks in, you don't even know it, and suddenly you realize it's not the wind in the leaves you hear, but rushing water.

The river was cut pretty deep into the rock, like a sluice with wide patches here and there and some places where fallen branches or whole trees snagged up a lot of debris. It was one of these trees we climbed down to get to the water. Madeleine looked at the river in both directions.

"Real good," she said. "I can fish all day here." Like a toast with a champagne glass, she held up the milk box full of worms she raised under the rabbit pens. "Guess you'll want to hike up a little higher and see if there's some flat space for your digging."

I nodded. It was pretty scrubbed-clean where we were standing. I pulled out the wide strip of shiny pink cloth we took from one of Mom's quilting bags. We always thought it was from a lady's slip. Madeleine climbed back up the log to tie it as high as she could. Our rule was that we'd gone too far off if we couldn't see the cloth.

Madeleine stood on her tiptoes in those faded overalls, stretched out like a great big piece of denim fruit. She tied off the cloth with a broad smile on her face. She was in her element and I knew she could live like that the rest of her life, fishing, driving a beat-up truck, never leaving Blue Falls.

"What do you get from collecting all them rocks and such," she said, looking down after she was satisfied the cloth would stay put.

"Stones," I corrected her. "It's not like Mom thinks. I'm not out here hunting pretty rocks. You know how she's always reading those books? It's the same thing when I find a bit of something worth keeping. There's a whole story involved I want to figure out."

Madeleine laughed. "I guess you see something in them rocks I don't. At least I can *eat* a trout." Then she kind of caught herself. "But don't get me wrong, Dez. We don't got a whole lot working in our favor, so do whatever makes you happy. Maybe you'll even dig up Glarney Polk's finger."

I walked upstream until I could barely see the pink strip. I don't know that I had to go as far as I did. It was all arbitrary. It just seemed natural that the farther away I was from Madeleine, the more likely I'd dig up something good. Of course, later I learned the best place to dig is right under people's feet.

I found a clearing a couple yards in from the river. I didn't have any idea what I was doing then, but maybe I have good instincts. The spot was slightly elevated. I know now it was a tumulus, but then it just seemed like the easiest place to dig. I was anything but scientific. I laid my screen on the ground and started shoveling the fairly loose, leaf-covered soil onto it. I picked up the screen and gave it a good shake, sifting the dirt until I was down to just leaves and sticks. It was a dry summer and that part of the process was pretty easy. It led me to nothing real fast. I kept going, though. Nowadays they don't call me until something's already been found. But I was tenacious enough to stick with it. I'd found a few arrowheads this way before, only I used a bucket with holes I'd punched in the bottom.

I was a couple hours into digging with no luck when my spade struck a rock. I brushed off a spot to see if it was one I would want. The stone wasn't too spectacular, but the fact I could clearly make out a letter "C" set me back on my ass for a few minutes. Just then I heard a splash below in the river. "That you, Madeleine?" I called out.

"Yep," she said. "These boots ain't much for walking on rocks. I'm gonna fish the pool up here a bit."

"Good," I said. But I was kind of mad. I felt like she might break whatever spell I was imagining.

I looked in the hole I dug and the grayish "C" was still there along with a little white chip where my spade hit. I started digging fast until I'd uncovered the face of the whole stone. It was about as big as a loaf of bread and read JACOB in crude lettering all the way across. I stepped back and took in the whole space, knowing I'd struck a grave.

Just then I heard Madeleine give out a huge grunt. "Desdemona get down here," she yelled.

I didn't want to leave. "What's the matter?"

"Just get down here." The way she said it, all garbled, I thought maybe something was wrong.

She was standing, struggling, her rod bent over completely, bobbing in every direction. I could only see the back of her, but she was obviously straining. I jumped down and ran to her side. "What do you want me to do?"

She looked at me, red faced, reeling in an inch, giving out two. I ran downstream to get her net. Just as I got back, the line snapped, sounding like the last air of a let-go balloon.

Madeleine leaned back on the rocks, startled. I knew that line breaking was probably the saddest thing she'd ever heard. "Hell," she said. "Just hell."

I stared at her.

"That thing musta been big as you," she said. And then she started laughing. "See why I love fishing?"

I calmly looked at her. "Come up and let me show you why I love digging," I said.

I told her I didn't want to dig around the marker any further. We needed to get some other people out there. Madeleine was good about it. In fact, it was her idea to tie the pink cloth near the spot so we could easily find it when we returned with someone.

It was the newspapers got me out of Blue Falls. I became the girl who'd found a surveyor from the 1800s. Whoever buried him included all his tools, though none of his documentation. I even got a scholarship promise if I finished high school.

II

Dad planned to run an apple orchard that was on the property. He moved us to Blue Falls from our place in Ponce de Leon, Missouri when I was thirteen. It was a long drive and I thought the truck Dad bought to haul all our belongings wouldn't make it. Most of the time Madeleine and I sat in the back with the few possessions Dad decided were worth moving—a mattress, our clothes. Mom's books which she had to insist on. Dad's tools.

The first couple of hours Madeleine and I didn't say a word to one another. We were both still a little shocked. A week earlier we were skinny-dipping in Skillet Creek and suddenly we were on the road to a whole new life. We were hunkered down out of the wind and surrounded by all our possessions.

"What do *you* think it's going to be like?" I finally said.

Madeleine rolled her eyes and her big dark freckles raised up with her cheeks. "Daddy says it's going to be perfect."

I already knew what Dad thought, so I gave her a stern look. "What do you think it's going to be like?"

"They eat lots of fish. And Mom says she heard it rains pretty much all the time up there."

It didn't sound like a place I wanted to go, but I also knew we didn't have much choice.

We ended up spending most of our trip looking out of the few open spaces in the truck. I propped my head between a wad of blankets and the mattress. Poking into my side was an old St. Louis parking meter Dad insisted we keep. For some reason, I'd always thought the whole United States looked like Ponce de

Leon, just endless miles of rolling hills covered in trees and an inch of topsoil. But after we were out of Missouri, everything got very flat and yellow for the longest time. Just fields occasionally broken up by stands of trees or single farmhouses.

Farther North, the more the land seemed to swell up and become greener, and the taller the trees got. I started wondering about what the rest of the world might be like.

III

I haven't been to the family home in Blue Falls in years. It's a big white farmhouse with a wraparound porch. All wood. I wasn't too happy when we moved to Washington, but when I saw where we'd be living, that I'd finally have my own room, I was excited.

I had a corner bedroom upstairs with two big windows that opened and shut with counterweights. From one side, I had a view of the rising hill behind us, and beyond that, the white-peaked Cascades. The window itself was crudely etched in one corner with the name *Caroline*.

The other window looked out on the apple orchard. As long as I lived there, the view was never the same. In winter it could look absolutely barren, black branches against the bright snow. In spring, if you walked through the trees during the blossoming, bees made the branches sound like high-voltage wires.

I don't think Dad ever asked Mom's opinion about any decision he made regarding the family. I guess she gave him a lot of leeway. He'd had a rough life. His own father, a man we were never allowed to meet, had cut off Dad's ear one drunken night.

The way Mom told it, when we were alone, was that Dad was about thirteen and our grandfather got mad at him for not doing some chore. It was just one of those bad moments when Dad decided to back-talk. And worse, he started walking away. Our grandfather, "sauced," as Mom used to say so politely, threw a plate at Dad's head, and there went the ear.

But, even though Dad was pretty rough around the edges and always trying to find his way, we knew he was making an effort. Getting us into that house was the best thing he ever did for any of us. Madeleine worked in the orchard and raised her rabbits. Between her worm farm and selling fryers, she set aside quite a bit of money for herself. Mom volunteered at the library. She did that back in Ponce de Leon too, but in Blue Falls it was so close she went a few days a week. And I rock hunted with a boy at school, Joe. His dad cut open the first geode I found. He helped me polish it so I could give it to Mom and Dad for their anniversary.

So all of us found something to do. What Dad got out of our moving, I suppose, was a happy family he could afford to feed and have a little extra, especially after he took the job at the dam.

The house kept us all happy. I always thought if I was going to raise a family, I'd want to do it in a house like that one. In the morning, the light came in over the wood floors and everything was tinted a warm yellow. And when it got hot in the summer, Mom opened up every window and the downstairs would catch the breeze and send it upstairs and out through the attic. I was happy but I still wanted more than that.

————ıllıı————

One time I found Dad sitting on the steps out front with his hands gripping the wood on either side of him. He was sitting there in his trademark blue-plaid shirt and overalls, staring off into nothing. He didn't even pay attention to the fact I sat next to him on his missing-ear side. I'd just had my fifteenth birthday and I was feeling like an adult. I tapped him on the shoulder. "Something on your mind?" I asked him.

He looked at me, surprised. "No, Mona," he said. He's the only one I ever let call me that. "But I got me a job today."

I didn't have to ask. None of us did. We knew we weren't making enough money on the orchard.

"I'm gonna work over in Bonneville on the dam."

He put his head down, which is as close to defeated as he ever showed any of us. Dad was a big man, square-jawed and red-skinned, like his body made so much blood it nearly ran out of space to keep it.

I knew exactly how to cheer him up. "Dad," I said. "Do we own this house?"

He sat up straight. "Down to the last nail."

I took his hand and walked him out into the driveway and we turned around. Then I decided to take a risk. I slapped him on the back and said, "That's a hell of a house."

"Goddamn. You're right, little girl," he said.

IV

Barlow made all my tools. If there was ever a man I might have married, it would've been him. He proposed while we were hunting for snapping turtles in Michigan. It was one of those rare summers when I wasn't working at a site. I was on sabbatical, so I took a few weeks for the two of us.

I'd known Barlow almost ten years by then. He was a metal worker and blacksmith I'd met when I was on a dig in New Mexico. He owned a shop just as Southwest was coming into fashion, so he had quite a business. That was a pretty wild period. I'd be in the ground all day and in his bed all night. He was a kick in the ass and every spare moment one of us got, we flew to where the other one was. More often than not, he came to me. I was working in the U.S. a lot back then.

Barlow planned a dream vacation for us that summer and all I could do was laugh when I saw our plane tickets to Michigan and he told me he'd rented a cabin on a swamp. He wasn't lying either. He fixed us up in the most dilapidated piece of crap I've ever seen. And I've been to a lot of countries.

We had to wear shoes inside because the floor was full of splinters. At night, the kerosene lamps shown through the outside walls and bugs flocked into the room. Of course, I wouldn't have traded that experience for anything.

It was the next to last day when everything kind of happened. I agreed to hunt turtles with Barlow. He'd been bothering me about it since we arrived. He led me off to a stream a mile or so away from the cabin. The brush was incredibly thick. Big as I am, Barlow is bigger and I walked behind him in the path his body created. "We'll have to do a tick-check tonight," he said.

"Is that what you call it?" I said.

Barlow turned around and offered a smile from his big square head. "They can get into the darndest places."

At the stream Barlow had us put on flannel shirts. "If these turtles get ahold of your flesh, you might lose a chunk," he said. "But they don't like flannel." He could barely get his on. His shoulders and biceps stretched the material every which way.

"Goddamn, you look good in that," I said.

The thing about catching snapping turtles, I learned, is that it's all tactile. The only visual element is looking for likely spots to search. Barlow showed me how we'd have to reach underwater, into the muddy banks and feel for the animals. You have to keep your hand flat and tight, otherwise a turtle might snap right through the webbing of your fingers. And you're searching for a tail because the turtles burrow in head first.

We slopped around in the water for a few hours with no luck, though I have to admit I loved the feel of the mud, how I could slide my hand into it like a warm knife through butter.

I was reaching under one bank right next to Barlow when I finally felt something unusual. As I kept going, I realized it was connected to his hand. I turned to him and he smiled. "Go ahead," he said and he pushed a square, fuzzy feeling thing into my hand under the water. When I pulled back, I was holding a mud-covered ring box, the blue felt barely visible. "Open it," he said.

"What are you doing, Barlow?" I asked even though I knew.

"Go ahead."

It was a gold ring with a turtle-shaped diamond setting. I sat back in the stream, squishing down into the silty bottom.

"Will you marry me, Dez? Come be with me in New Mexico."

I knew my answer right away. "Well, hell," I said. "I can't."

Barlow looked surprised. His large blue eyes widened and then pinched up. "Why not?"

"Hell, Barlow," I said. "I move around too much. I'm never home."

I loved Barlow, but I never thought I could marry him. "There's just too much to uncover," I told him. It's a hard thing to explain, but I tried. I explained what it's like to be down in the ground twenty feet or a hundred. You're immersed in the sial layer and suddenly there's the tip of an ax or even a kitchen midden. Or you brush away the earth and you're confronted with a human femur thousands of years old.

Barlow sat up on his knees and swished his dirty hands in the water.

I handed him the ring box. "It's beautiful," I said. "But there's that moment you're standing in the middle of a dig and you see a coating of dust on your own body and you realize the earth is swallowing you too and you don't have much time."

Barlow scooted himself up on the bank. "What about having a family. Don't you want to be around people you love?"

"The people I love understand."

"Really? When was the last time you saw your sister and mother?"

"Quite a while. But I'll get back there some day. Maybe even retire in Blue Falls."

Barlow shook his head. "It isn't any good if you make it home in time for all the funerals."

V

The lecture in Ann Arbor was over. I'd given a talk about preserving the cliff dwellings in Arizona. The complicated nature of tourism, respecting Native Americans, and preserving sites of archaeological and anthropological significance. People applauded. They always do.

Mother's funeral had been that same morning. Madeleine refused to wait until I could get home. I had talked to her three days before the speech in one of those rare moments we spoke over the phone. "If you cared about Momma at all," she said, "you'd of come when I told you she was dying."

"Dammit, Madeleine," I said, "that was a month ago. Was I supposed to freeze in place? I can come Friday but not Thursday. There are a hundred people here, professionals, counting on my speech."

"Your sister is counting on you." With that, she hung up.

I was alone for a late dinner of cheap house-wine and pizza after the lecture and reception. The walk back to my hotel took me by campus. I was thinking about Mom and how proud she'd be of where I'd gotten. And I was upset with Madeleine for not holding the funeral for me just one day.

An icy blanket of snow dulled under the blunt light of a half moon. I sat on a bus bench. Am I wrong, I wondered. Then I heard a flutter and gurgling from high in the tall trees across the street. Dozens and dozens of spadelike forms rested among the branches, crows, thick as leaves. One jumped to a new perch, its wings angled out like saw blades against the night sky then refolded into a solid drop of blackness.

———||||||———

These memories roil and ferment unnoticed, untested. Desdemona does not go home after receiving in Xi'an the letter from her sister. That won't happen for years, not until London. She will be crouched in an excavation pit where they've uncovered Roman ruins. As usual, she will be keeping busy, pressing forward, putting distance between herself and anything that isn't now. Here, her advice is needed on extracting entire stone walls from the soil. Procedure. Preservation. "Goddamn you people are in a hurry," she will say, looking at the frantic excavation in the dark soil. "Goddamn."

It will be a cool day in the city, rain in the morning, then bright sun from the freshly scrubbed sky. The sun will creep below the buildings, the woody smell of hot chestnuts floating over the excavation. "Time to knock off, Desdemona?" one of the workers will yell. And she will smile, because she is not in charge here. She is merely a consultant, but it's a common mistake. Desdemona will shrug and point to her colleague who already has his hands on his hips. "All right then," he will say. "That's enough for today. Get back to your families and whatnot."

And it's just that phrase, after all these years that will catch Desdemona off-guard. She will be stilled by the memory of Madeleine's eventual forgiveness for not coming home for their mother's funeral. She will recall Madeleine's long ago request that she come home to Blue Falls. She will consider, too, this excavation which whispers secrets in her ear, the orange tile from a Roman roof she holds, a firm thing in her hand, slightly wet, something she understands. A fact. This city, she will think, the whole of it, is heaped up on the shoulders of history. She will hold the terra-cotta shard because the archaeologists have questions and she must have answers. It will be here when I come back, she will tell herself, surprised by the revelation. Going home to Madeleine has always seemed a distant option, but as she watches the workers putting away their tools, she will decide she must go home as well. It will be a surprise for Madeleine and that will make everything okay, she will tell herself.

Desdemona will leave London for Blue Falls. It will occur to her it has been nearly three years since she and her sister last communicated. She will drive all the way from the airport in Seattle, through the cedar- and birch-lined roads which have changed little since she left so many years ago. She will drive alongside the fattened Columbia, the denseness of water that isn't really a river any longer. The sky will be filmy with cumulus, the sun weak and larval.

She will slow to read a rust-pocked sign, hand-painted, shot through with bullet holes. *Welcome to Blue Falls* it will say over an illustration of the famous landmark. She will imagine her town a ruin like this dilapidated sign, but a smile will come across her face and she will be surprised that she is happy to finally come home. She has seen Madeleine just twice in the last ten years, both times in the city, and just for a quick dinner before leaving the country again.

She will think of the big white house she spent so many years in, how Madeleine has stayed in it all this time. She will think of the heavy windows with their wavy glass, of the creaking stairs, that fourth step she and Madeleine had to avoid when they went out for a late-night sip of the applejack they fermented down by the spring. She will remember her father taught them how to make it in the first place. Daddy to Madeleine, Dad to Desdemona. And he'd be real proud of me, she will think. And even though they're older now, she's gotten home in time, she will tell herself. It will all work out. And there's so much to tell, all the countries she's lived in, the people she's met. And maybe Barlow would finally get it too if he could see her now, making it home just like she said she would. Maybe it is time to come home to stay, she will think. The world can do without me. Maybe if I settle down here, I'll have Barlow and his family up here one summer, all seven of them, fishing and rock hunting and swimming, just like me and Madeleine used to do. There's plenty of time to make up for being gone so long, she will decide.

She will drive past Madeleine's diner, amazed that it is still open, that this town itself with its little brick shops and their cluttered windows has actually changed, now a wine and cigar store, a coffeehouse, one business that simply says *Outdoor Needs and Lingerie,* all on River Street planted with young trees; people, tourists perhaps, walking along wide strips of new red brick. So much will be different. It's the perfect time to come home after all, she will think. I've been away much too long.

She will turn onto Sturgeon Road and look up the hill at the blockade of spruce that marks her home. She will feel her blood pushing faster through her body. Just beyond those trees is the house, and poor Madeleine. But Desdemona will know it will be okay in a moment. She will be home and they can sit on the porch and have iced tea and talk, and even if it turns out Madeleine's upset, she can tell her sister how much she loves her, that she never really forgot her in all this time. She just had to go out and be a part of the world. Make her mark, her petroglyph, her cuneiform, lay her tools out there to be found years from now. Madeleine will understand this, Desdemona will tell herself.

As she drives up closer to her home, she will think she's made a mistake. There will be a yellow, double-wide trailer almost where there should be a house, *her* house. She will look at the address, stunned as she pulls into the familiar gravel drive in front of the trailer sitting at an angle just to the side of the charred remnants of the house, overgrown with weeds and opportunistic saplings. Desdemona will get out of the car. Most of the burned wood will have been removed, part of the porch flooring remaining along with the front steps and the bannister, as if it's leading up to the entranceway to an invisible dwelling. She will walk through the years-old rubble, stirring the ground with her boot, picking up a metal spoon, a melted comb, a single clear marble, things she does not recognize, things she will toss down.

She will walk to the trailer, upset that Madeleine has never said anything about this. The metal steps leading to the door will make a hollow clang under her boots. She will knock but there will be no immediate answer. She will knock again and pick up the newspapers littered around her feet. The newest one will be days old. Desdemona will knock again and call out Madeleine's name. No answer. She will turn around and look beyond the burned house, at the slope of Blue Falls that ends at the Columbia. Across the road, she will see a woman dressed entirely in brown coming out of the old Buckle place. The woman will hold her hand over her eyes to block the sun and look at Desdemona. Her hand will fall and her body stiffen with a jolt, but she will manage a broad, friendly wave. She will close her door and walk down her brick pathway to the road where she will turn toward Desdemona.

As she gets closer, Desdemona will see the woman is wearing a uniform with a badge. The woman will stop halfway up the hill to light a cigarette. She will take a long drag and when she does, Desdemona will see the still look on her face.

Desdemona will walk to the driveway next to her car, indurate memories crowding forward. She will consider the burned ruins of her old house, and beyond that, the apple orchard with its dead rows, a few trees holding on, wild and spindly. The air will feel calcified, dry and thin in her lungs. She will steady herself on the car, waiting for the woman coming up the road, waiting for her to say what Desdemona suddenly fears, that she has come home too late.

Drawings
by Andrew Warhol

————||||||||————

Maybe you're reading this in a doctor's office or maybe it came right to your home and you're sitting at the kitchen table with a cup of decaf, or hot tea with a half-squeezed wedge of lemon, I don't know. The point is I've got a story for you, a big one, something you have to sit down for. And it's not one of those secondhand kind where all the details get changed around and it turns out later the guy wasn't hit by car at all—he was struck by a little girl on a bike, or something like that. No, this story happened to me and it's all true, the sharks, the gun, Gil. It's a tall tale from your backyard and I'm telling you all the parts they didn't report in the newspapers.

————||||||————

147

It's always a problem where to start, but maybe you got to know about me, like I was right before I met Gil. I mean *right before*. So I'm going to tell it like this. It's autumn in Los Angeles. I'm watching a low, amber sky. There are wildfires in Malibu again and the sun drops through the smoke like an orange marble in dark syrup. These are the sunsets I like best, created by Santa Ana winds and someone with good timing. Sometimes I wonder if pyromaniacs practice.

I'm waiting in my car in the parking lot of the grocery store where I work. I time the start of my shift by the light left in the sky. I'm thinking of quitting. In a month I'll be married, in two months I'll be thirty-six. Being the night manager isn't the job I want for the rest of my life. I thought about joining the LAPD, thought about it so long that now I'm too old. I reach into the back of my car and grab a maroon tie that hasn't been unknotted for two weeks. I slip the loop over my neck and adjust it beneath my oxford blue collar.

Outside my car, I'm immersed in the woody smell of smoke and yellowed wild fennel that grows in vacant lots. The only way Los Angeles will change, I think, is if it burns.

Halfway across the parking lot someone calls my name. It's Gil, only I don't know that yet because we've never met. He is walking directly behind me. I stop and turn. Gil is tall. His clothes are wrinkled and dirty. He wears a green cotton army jacket with a "Seattle" patch stitched on the shoulder. His blonde hair is pulled back in a ponytail. Even though I don't know him, I'm not surprised Gil knows my name. That's why the store makes me wear it on a tag.

Gil holds a large shoulder bag out to me. The brown-and-orange Aztec patterns are distorted by angular contents. "Those fuckers won't let me take my bag inside," Gil says. "I told them you'd vouch for me." Later, I will forget to tell the police about the bag, about its contents and the fact that Gil liked books.

"I don't even know you," I say.

"I've been in the last two nights on your shift. I buy macaroons to feed the pigeons." Gil holds out the shoulder bag again, looking a bit surprised I don't know him. "My name is Gil," he says.

"So you're the Macaroon Man they've been talking about." For two weeks now the checkers have been discussing Gil and how he always buys a dozen packages of macaroons. It bothers me, the fact that I've missed Gil every time. I don't miss much, not in this store, not on my shift, not after working here so long. I take the bag from Gil and look inside. All I see are books. I read the spine of the top copy, *The Poems and Written Addresses of Mary T. Lathrap*. "So, what do you want me to do?"

Gil smiles. His teeth are surprisingly white and straight. "Just tell them I'm cool. They'll listen. I'm running out of macaroons."

I hand Gil his shoulder bag. "I don't even know you. And, to be honest, I'd just as soon the pigeons starved."

"Look," Gil says. His voice rattles like there are small beads tumbling in his throat. "The way I see it, you're the only stand-up manager in there. You have to help me."

I think about the customers who come in late at night with snakes twined around their necks, of the male rockers in black skirts and women who wear knives in brown leather cases on their hips. And it's true, I think, I'm the only manager who knows what he's doing. A bag of books is the least of my worries. "Come in later tonight," I say, turning and walking toward the store. And that right there is the moment I let Gil into my life, that little decision that flipped everything all around. And I promise I'm getting to the part about the sharks real soon.

Gil comes in a little after midnight. He's changed his clothes and shaved. He has on a white sweatshirt that says *Las Vegas* in red letters, and pants half a size too small. He holds up his shoulder bag for me to see, a bit triumphant, walking toward the cookie section.

I'm not thinking about Gil, the Macaroon Man. I'm counting money at the front desk. I'm not thinking about that either, though. I'm thinking about the folded-up list in my back pocket. These are the responsibilities I have for the wedding and a timeline that my fiancée, Kay, has written out for me. If it were a small wedding, everything would be done by now.

The next thing on the list is hiring a band. Kay's directions are explicit. No hard rock or folk music. They must be able to play dance music, including slower songs for the older guests. It occurs to me that we've thought more about the music for the reception than our vows. Sometimes I think I won't hire anyone at all. Would it be less of a wedding? What if everyone danced to music they imagined in their heads? I think of a dance floor of silent tempos, couples waltzing, line-dancing, swinging, and freestyling. So much easier.

Gil shakes his bagful of macaroon packages to get my attention. "I'm all hooked up, brother."

I slide the money I'm counting into a drawer and lock it before I turn.

"I knew you'd come through," Gil says.

"I just let you spend money."

"It's more than that. You sized me up. You should've been a cop."

I wince a laugh but say nothing.

Gil smiles, circles of freckles rising on his bony cheeks. He reaches out to shake my hand—a tan, veiny offering that hangs between us in the fluorescent light.

After a moment, I acquiesce. Gil's hand is warm and firm.

"Let's talk after you get off," Gil says. "Maybe get waffles?"

"Can't. I'll be here for a while."

Gil shakes his head. "You're off at one. Another hour. I asked."

"I've got stuff to do."

"You'll go home and eat cold cereal. Turn on the TV." Gil smiles and shrugs an apology as if he's hurt my feelings. "That's what I imagine people like you do."

I roll a pen between my fingers like a baton. I don't like customers getting too familiar, especially the strange ones. I don't like anyone getting too familiar. "Maybe I was wrong about you. You're starting to sound like a dick." This isn't how to treat customers, I know that, but sometimes I have to with the crazy ones, show authority, stake out ground. And the store is definitely my ground.

Gil opens his shoulder bag and stuffs his macaroons on top of a book with a blue-and-red cover and faded gold lettering. "We're a lot alike. I size people up, too. But we'll make it another time. I've got to find someone to give me a ride to work tonight anyway."

"I wouldn't come back," I say.

"Have to. You guys are the only ones that carry this brand." He holds up the macaroons proudly as he walks away.

You know how I was feeling, like I was the only normal person alive. Like I was the glue that held the world together. But I knew what that meant right away because I'm the type of person that would say "He seems normal," when what I really mean is that the guy in question is boring. But I was right about one thing because boring people are the glue for the rest of society, the people that have nothing to do but create rules, follow them, and make sure everyone else follows them, too. And if that was the definition, I did indeed feel like glue, a big sticky glob of it, getting married like I was supposed to, counting other people's money day after day, making sure there was nothing new in my life.

The next night I warn the security guard about Gil. As my shift progresses, I'm actually disappointed Gil hasn't tried to come in. I tell the security guard I'd like to kick Gil out myself. Twice, I check the cookie aisle just to make sure. Toward the end of the night, I hear my name over the intercom and run up front. I'm thinking maybe Gil has stolen something, maybe he's resisting and we can throw his ass in jail. But when I get to the front of the store, all I find is the security guard holding a bent-over old man, one of my regulars. "He's got vodka and OJ this time," the security guard says.

"Leo, give us the stuff back," I say. I know where it's hidden and don't really want the recovery job. We've been doing this for years. It's these sideshows I'm famous for handling. Leo undoes his pants, hands shaking, and stands. "I don't know how many more times we can do this," I say. I slide the liquor and juice out from underneath the fold of Leo's wet, distended belly. He leans into me and mumbles something I can't make out. I put my ear closer to Leo's mouth so I can hear him. He repeats himself, a day's worth of alcohol souring his breath. "Not tonight," I say, and then louder, "Can't give you a ride tonight." Normally I would but Kay has told me to stop giving strangers rides home. I look at my employees as the security guard escorts Leo outside. "Super Manager strikes down another freak," one of them says.

I shake my head. "Careful. Freaks spend money, too." I turn and watch the security guard put Leo in a cab, the awkwardness of it, Leo trying to bend at the waist to slide into the back seat. How does it come to that, I wonder. When, if ever, do you see who you are becoming? I watch Leo struggle into the taxi and try to imagine who he may have been before he became a lonely old man of few words.

I decide to leave a half-hour early. I walk slowly to my car. Even though it's late, it's not dark. The city lights turn the sky the color of scrubbed pewter. The fires in Malibu are not out yet, but the winds have changed direction, so the air is clearing. I find this freshness disturbing. I've gotten used to a Los Angeles of hard smells. Somehow, the scent of spent fuel and neglected jasmine feel more indigenous.

Leaving the store is always uncomfortable because it forces a realization which has gotten stronger, that out here I am not a manager. Out here, I am simply Dave. Just Dave. Dave Jackson. Tonight, I stop walking for a moment and weigh the currency of my name. I say it out loud. I stand in the center of the parking lot, occupying a tiny space in a large city. Is this my allotment, I wonder, the width of two size-nine shoes? Dave Jackson, Kay's fiancée.

Walking toward my car, I notice someone sitting on the trunk. Gil.

"Sorry I didn't make it in, brother. I sold my wheels to some illegal aliens for a hundred bucks. I had to take the bus all the way from the valley." Gil lightly works something small between his fingers.

"What the hell are you doing on my car?" I undo my tie and the top button of my collar. I stand right next to Gil, who simply smiles.

"I'm keeping a child alive in Africa." He holds up a rolled cigarette. "Ginger, cloves, and bone. I learned this in Seattle. I made one for each of us." He offers me the cigarette.

"No thanks. And get off my car."

Gil's features tighten and his eyes close slightly. "You're too uptight. Take a cigarette. I'm gonna change your life."

"I don't smoke bone."

"You don't even know what kind it is."

I unlock my car door and throw my tie inside. The smell of fast-food containers wafts out. "This is why everyone thinks you're crazy, Gil. You say crap like that."

Gil slides off the trunk, his shoulder bag clunking on the bumper. "You said my name." He stares into my eyes as if he were about to say something important. "I need a ride."

I get in my car without answering, but Gil catches the door.

"Don't take off on me, brother," Gil says. His voice sounds

vulnerable. He holds the car door firmly. "I'm just asking for a ride. You like sharks?"

Gil's eyes are like dark stones in the dim light.

"Sharks?"

"Are you scared of me?" Gil asks.

Suddenly the air feels compressed and purple. I'm aware of my own breath and the pulse at the tip of my fingers. What's the difference between Gil out here and Gil in the store? I see the shoulder bag and remember. This is a man who carries books and buys macaroons for pigeons. "I'm not scared," I say, and step out of the car. Gil backs up. "But look at all the weird crap you do—out of the blue you're asking for a ride and talking about sharks."

"Context," Gil says as an almost teacherly reminder. "I was normal. I was practically you. But that didn't get me far."

"So, exactly where are you now?"

"Moment to moment, brother. Right now I'm working for the government. Top secret. And all I'm saying now is I sold my car and I need a ride to make my shift on time."

"The government, Gil? Come on." I roll my ring around my finger, a gift from Kay. I'm still unused to the smoothness of the gold even though I have worn it for two years. She gave it to me when we moved in together.

"Holy shit," Gil says. "Are you married?"

"Engaged," I say, recognizing the monotone of my own reply.

"Then I met you just in time. I was married. She died, though. Rough stuff, brother."

I look into Gil's face, the new sadness of it. "Sorry to hear that."

"She was the one. I mean, *the* one. Yours too?"

I look at my ring and then at Gil. I think of the wedding, of Kay, her active blue eyes and calm lips, her blonde hair and white skin, freckled over the nose. "We'll see." I lean back on the car, crossing my arms. Gil joins me.

"You never answered, by the way," Gil says.

"What?"

"You like sharks or not? I'm training them for the government. You got to swear not to tell anyone. We put these magnetic bombs on their backs and train them to attach themselves to ship hulls. I'm involved in some heavy shit."

I kind of laugh. Gil is crazy but not crazy "mad," I decide. "Right, Gil. You train sharks."

He stands in front of me, his white teeth gleaming, sharp looking in the halogen light of the parking lot. "Okay, Okay," he says. "I'm not the trainer. I just assist. I'm not an icthyologist or anything. I just lucked into it. If you give me a ride, I'll show you." Gil takes a place next to me on the car again, staring off into space. He tells me a lot of things I didn't know about sharks and corrects some stuff I thought I knew. He talks for a long time, telling me how he won't eat the meat because sharks urinate through their skin, how not all of them have to keep swimming to stay alive. He shows me a scar on his forearm he says is a shark bite, a "nip" he calls it. He tells me all about how the government isn't using dolphins anymore because it isn't PC. "But sharks, nobody cares about sharks," he says. He tells me about a membrane that covers a shark's eyes as it bites into its prey and about the seventy-thousand-gallon tanks where they do all their training. When he's done, we're quiet for a few minutes. He's crazy but he knows what he's talking about.

I'm still fooling with my ring.

"That sounds like a problem," Gil says, pointing to the ring.

I try to think of something to say, but that's the truth of it. "Well, you know," I finally manage.

Gil turns and shakes his head. "Forget the ride. You wouldn't be much fun," and then, "You're just one of the hive," he says in quiet accusation.

The hive, I understand, is Los Angeles. I think of the white box in my neighbor's backyard, the bees crawling all over each other at the small slit of an entrance. Once, my neighbor showed me the constant procession of bees flying in and out and the little pile of debris, dead bees, in front of each hive. We watched a group pull and push a dead member over the edge. That's how it is, I think now, looking at the store, considering Kay. That's how I'll end up, on the pile, without ever having broken away.

I look at Gil and the shoulder bag sitting at his feet. "Hand me one of those bone cigarettes," I say.

I would have given Gil a ride that night but he didn't ask again. We just finished our cigarettes and he left. And to tell you the truth, I was disappointed. I was never one to do anything out of the ordinary. I wanted to see those sharks, and even if there weren't any, Gil, at least, was something new. Instead, I went home and kissed Kay on her forehead while she slept, poured a bowl of cereal, and watched a food dehydrator infomercial.

Days pass before I find Gil sitting on the trunk of my car again after work. "Give me a lift?" he says. He wears a dark blue jump suit, like a uniform, and I guess he can tell I'm looking because he says "Work," tugging on his collar.

In fifteen minutes we're headed for Riverside County, East on Interstate 10, not out to the ocean where I would've assumed. Gil reminds me it's all top secret. "We got the whole place laid out like catfish ponds," he says, patting his shoulder bag which is lumped between us.

Actually, this is not unusual. Sometimes, after work, I drive the freeways before I go home. I unroll my window and feel the changes in heat. The way the Hollywood freeway slouches between the hills and sinks into the compressed air of the valley or how the landscape along the 405 freeway changes from the smell of decaying asphalt to salt air. This is the only way I can reassure myself that Los Angeles is not a giant fissure into which all ubiquity has collapsed.

"Now that we're out on the road, I should warn you," Gil says after a long silence. "I'm a serial killer."

I smile and laugh. I laugh until Gil joins in. "Are you going to beat me to death with your books?" I ask. The inside of the car is streaked with white and red light from cars passing and falling back. Me and Gil laugh into another silence that lasts for minutes.

"What kind of bone is in those cigarettes?" I finally ask.

"What?"

"I never asked you what kind of bone."

"Human." Gil sounds serious.

"No, really."

"To do it right, they have to be human."

"Enough of that creepy shit."

Gil chuckles. "To tell the truth, I got mine from an herbalist and who knows what's in it. I'm probably smoking chalk."

I feel Gil waiting for a response. "So, the sharks," I say. "You going to show them to me?"

"Sure, brother. You'll be sick of sharks you'll see so many. We got this Great White, a baby. They die in captivity. But they raised this one from an egg sac and they're thinking maybe its gonna make it. Four feet long and growing."

"Cool," I say, and it's about all I can do to hide my excitement, which is funny because as a kid, after the divorce, my father used to take me to Marine Land about once a month and I hated it.

We've been driving for a while. "Maybe we should get something to eat," Gil says. "Pull off at the next offramp." He fumbles through his bag and retrieves the blue-and-red book from a few days ago.

I look for restaurant signs but all I see are gas stations. It occurs to me I've never run out of gas in all the time I've lived in Los Angeles. "There's nothing here," I say.

"Of course there is. A coffee shop." Gil thumbs through his book. "You could take every offramp from here to New York. There's always a coffee shop." Gil leans over, his finger pointing to a recipe for curried lobster. "I want to order this," he says.

I realize what the book is. "You can't walk into a restaurant and order out of your own cookbook."

"This is *Amy Vanderbilt's Complete Cookbook*. It's a bible."

I shrug. "I'm not really hungry."

"I have a few macaroons left, I guess." Gil puts the book away.

He turns the overhead light on, the two of us dim and sudden ghosts in the passenger window.

Kay likes to do this, turn the light on while I'm driving. She reads or sometimes puts on makeup. It's uncomfortable, not because it's distracting, but because people in other cars can see in so clearly. Usually I shut off the light, but this time I let Gil go, watch him put on a Colorado Rockies baseball cap, threading his ponytail through the back. He doesn't come up with any macaroons.

Just before Gil turns off the light, I settle on our vague outlines in the side passenger window. It's as if the world is passing through us. The lights and concrete, the oleander on the periphery sifting through me and Gil as if we are inconsequential obstacles. The first time I saw Kate was at a film-festival benefit for AIDS research. She walked across the lobby carrying two glasses of wine. Her direction was clear and I was between her and her destination. At the last moment, I stepped out of her way. She didn't acknowledge me and never missed a step.

"So why are you getting married?" Gil says as he snaps off the light.

"We've been together five years," I say. It's an easy answer.

"But *why?*"

I know I should say I love Kay, but something else comes out. "We're functional." We are deep into suburban Los Angeles County, the center of its pathology. The hills are black mounds speckled with bright colors. On either side, the avenues glare with moving headlights thick as serum. They inject themselves between homes, tract after tract. It makes me think of broken glass.

"You're a mess, brother," Gil says. He unrolls his window and leans back against the door. The car is filled with wind. "I bet you don't like your job either."

I crack my window open as well. "Not really."

"You're a bus driver."

"What are you talking about?" I say.

"You're like a bus driver for an elementary school field trip. Everyone goes inside to the art exhibit or the Archeology Museum and you stay on your bus. Maybe you sit there with a little fan blowing on you. Maybe you lean against the bus while you smoke a cigarette, but you never go inside. You don't even consider it. You know your yellow bus with black stripes and green vinyl seats and that's good enough."

"You don't know anything about me." The car rattles over a set of lane reflectors and I correct my steering. The lights on the side of the interstate come farther apart now. Tractor-trailers dominate the slow lane, the sound of their tires a constant and ominous hum. My jaw tightens. "Look at you. No family. No car. Asking me for a two-hour ride home. And you criticize my life?"

Gil sits up straight. He pulls his bag close to him and looks at me, one hand on the dash, the other over the seat back. "We need to take the 15 South," he says, pointing to a sign. He sharpens his voice. "I have a degree in Library Science. Two years ago I was firing pottery in Blue Falls, Washington. A year ago I was working at a casino in Las Vegas. I had a wife when I was twenty-six. She died. Nothing poetic. I came home from the library one night and she was lying on the floor of our kitchen. Aneurism." He sits back and takes off his cap. "That's a life."

The two of us remain silent. I look straight ahead. It's nearly three A.M. We've been driving a long time. Freeway lines shoot by us like comets. This is the stretch of Interstate 15 between San Diego and San Bernadino—desert, and foothills, and dairies. It's a nearly black corridor. I drive eighty miles per hour. I want to get Gil to work and I'm ready to see some sharks.

Other cars on the road come fast and in packs. Nothing—then six or seven pairs of headlights advancing, passing, becoming dissipating red dots. A gray lump ahead interrupts the dividing lines. "Dead dog," I say, veering slightly.

Gil twists around. "It's alive."

In the rearview mirror the body is darker. It raises one end. I look ahead, thinking *Do not stop.*

"Pull over. Pull over," Gil yells.

I slow and stop on the shoulder. Gil jumps out. We've gone too far to see the dog. I click on my hazards, allowing anemic strobes of yellow into the moonless night. The smell of cattle yards falls like incense as I step out of the car and walk the edge of the freeway. Before I can see Gil or the dog, I hear heavy, clipped expellations of air.

I follow the grunts of the dog, looking for it and Gil in the near–pitch dark. And then I am upon them, a bull terrier, on the line, one lane out from where Gil stands at the edge of the freeway. It is up on its forelegs, trying to move, weighted by an immobile lower half. I see round silver tags, blood running from the dog's mouth and pooled like mercury on the pavement. It's going to die, I'm sure.

"A vet," Gil yells. "Give me your keys. I'll back up the car. It's too big to carry."

I say nothing. Gil snatches the keys out of my hand and disappears into the dark between the yellow blinking lights. Maybe it isn't as bad off as it looks. I'm saying this to myself but I know the dog is going to die.

The car rumbles back and I help Gil spread papers and an old shirt on the back seat. A faint shifting light enters the car, and then I hear them, engines and tires making sounds like swarming insects. Gil rushes out to the dog and crouches down to scoop him up but quickly backs off when the headlights hit him. I watch the oncoming traffic and Gil fidgeting at the edge. It is all out of our hands.

I fix on the dog. First a few cars pass, all of them blue in the night. They stay to the edge of their lanes to miss the dog. The asphalt vibrates beneath me as they pass. The dog strains but does not move. The first sets of cars completely pass and for a moment, the world is still as forgotten freight.

In the seconds-long break of traffic, I realize I'm mad at the dog for not getting hit. It should be over, I think. I run out to Gil, who is surprisingly motionless, arms crossed. The dog begins to move as the second group of headlights approach. There is a jacked-up Toyota truck cutting a hazy aura in the darkness. I expect this or the motor home directly behind it to hit the dog. But it remains untouched as the sawlike sound of tires fades away.

We run out to the dog, bending down to pick it up. It's quivering and cold. I know that it's half dead but Gil seems determined. Maybe there's a vet who could help but I doubt it.

"How should we do this?" Gil asks. It's the first time he's ever seemed unsure of anything.

A car horn blares. We've forgotten about the freeway. It's an extended blast from a white Cadillac, backing us into the fourth lane. The bull terrier raises itself as high as it can go. My lips tighten as the Cadillac begins to change lanes to miss the dog. It does not complete the move. The driver flicks on the brights and straddles his car over the same line as the dog. Gil reaches out like he's going to help but I hold him back.

The Cadillac slams the dog with the point of its grillwork, the white machine hiding the animal beneath it, then spitting it out the back end, flesh sliding fast like something fallen off a luggage rack. It rolls to the shoulder, halted by its softened legs. "Fuck," Gil screams, running.

When I reach Gil and the dog, the night is nearly silent again. The only sound is the fractional click of the hazard lights. The black sky is heavy with stars. I touch Gil's shoulder. What do you do with a lifeless thing? What *can* you do? We walk back to the car. For a moment we sit, staring at the animal, which has reverted to its original image, a gray form in the distance, dead dog.

We pull back onto the freeway. The image of the dog being hit replays itself slower in my mind and somehow I think I need to comfort Gil. "It wouldn't have lived," I tell him. "There would've been a couple more hours of pain and they would've put it to sleep."

"It was *trying*." Gil turns to me. "Just like you deciding to give me a ride. Pathetic, but trying. Do you want me to be your white Cadillac?"

I turn to the road. "What the hell does that mean? You act as if you're doing me some kind of favor. Who's giving who a ride, Gil?"

"I work over there," Gil says, agitated. He points to a distant set of lights, a smudge of brightness vague as an inconclusive x-ray.

I turn on the radio, hoping music will fill the moment. The dial rolls across the FM line. Nothing but scratchy music fading in and out. The AM side is nearly the same and then, finally, garbled voices, a call-in show. I tune them in as closely as possible but I can't make out a thing.

"There's a coincidence. They're talking about me," Gil says. "They're always talking about me." He reaches into his shoulder bag. "That bastard in the car deserves worse than the dog." He pulls out a gun. "Wish I had this out."

"What the hell are you doing with that?" I stop the car. "Get out."

Gil's jaws clench. "I need to get to work. We're not far. Keep going."

"Get out."

Gil points the gun at me. "No, really," he says, "keep going."

We drive a bit before we come to the entrance of Gil's work, a dirt drive under a dusty billboard that reads "Goddard's Year-Round Fishing." It has a picture of a boy saying "I want 'em all." His tongue is out and he's pulling a catfish from a lake. Only someone has painted a woman's body over the fish with flesh-colored paint. I look at the distorted cartoon of a woman, trying to notice everything, the gun still pointed at me. But in a strange way I'm relieved, or vaguely hopeful, because these are the catfish lakes

Gil talked about, the whole top-secret cover for the shark program. And I'm thinking at least there will be people around and we can do something about Gil.

"So this is where you work." I turn the car slowly into the driveway. I've taken so many turns I don't know where I am. We pull up to a long building, a motel. There are no cars or lights. I flick on my brights. The building is pink or orange, I can't tell. I think about jumping out and running when I stop the car...but the gun. Gil directs me to the second to last door.

"Kind of freaky, huh, brother?" Gil laughs.

As Gil searches his bag for a key, I look for a sign of other people, try to orient myself. I don't see the slightest hint of shark tanks, which by now I'm not really expecting. I notice the smell of the lake, or the cattails rather, and the scent of wild sage. The mix sours the air. It reminds me of when I was seven and I caught crawdads for a bait and tackle store. Four cents apiece for each one under three inches. There were two methods, bacon tied on one end of a string and dropped into their tiny mudholes or a pencil for the larger ones. Either way, they rarely let go. I look at Gil, the gun still pointed right at me, like a too-big crawdad I can't shake off.

"Come on." Gil directs me with the gun.

"Is this more of that crazy shit like the bone-smoking?" I'm suddenly hopeful it's that simple as we walk toward the room. "I should get back," I try.

Gil unlocks the door and flips on a light. "It's all crazy shit." He looks past me. "A couple families come out here on weekends. Teenagers used to drink beer here at night until I showed up."

Gil holds the door for me. It's a large room. There's a kitchenette with a hot plate and quarter-sized refrigerator. Across from the bed are an orange loveseat and a dresser, the imitation wood veneer separating at the sides.

"Sit down," Gil says.

"I should get back," I say again, turning toward Gil, who is not smiling.

"No, really. Sit." Gil points to the loveseat, holding me with gesture.

I sit straight up, fighting off a nervous shake as I reach for my wallet. "Why don't you take this and let me go?"

"You don't get it, brother." Gil stiffens. "This is not a robbery."

"Then what do you want?"

Gil sits on the edge of the bed and I stare at the weapon, at the strong hand holding it. "Turn on the radio," Gil says. He points with his gun. "Find that talk show we had on in the car."

I search for the station. The reception is slightly better. The voice is heavy with static and still I can't make out any of the words.

"Murder in Las Vegas. Ballistics and matching bullets," Gil says as if he's hearing exactly what's being said. "I told you they were talking about me. They don't have a nickname yet. I'm not flashy enough. But Las Vegas was number twelve. Took 'em until today to figure out it was me. Three fucking weeks."

Gil's words come fast. He talks about all the people he's killed. He starts pacing. A moth flicks around the inside of the lamp next to the bed. I try to remember what day it is, what month. I decide it's Tuesday, it is October. It is fall, the time of year when offices decorate their walls with artificial autumn leaves. Suddenly I think of a band to hire for the wedding.

"Why are you smiling?" Gil asks. He sits next to me, still holding the gun. "You should be scared shitless."

I say nothing but my muscles are tightly drawn. There are clothes heaped in the corner of the room and on the nightstand, a rotary phone with red-and-white service buttons. No sudden movements, I think. Late night nature-shows replay in my head. If a shark attacks, you gouge its eyes with your thumb. You play dead if it's a bear. What do you do at gunpoint?

"I'm still hungry," Gil says. "Do you want something?"

I shake my head no. I think about how I got here. I broke my own rules, went off the path. I see Gil standing in the store with his sack of macaroons, then sitting on the back of my car rolling cigarettes. What was I thinking? I remember standing in the parking lot and that small space I stood on and how much larger my allotment seems at this moment. "Why are you doing this?" I ask, finally.

Gil walks to the kitchenette. "You should thank me. This is the ride of your life." Gil points the gun directly at my head. "Put your hand over your chest." I feel my heart shaking my body. The room is suddenly bright and singed, like the heat glaring off white sand. "I need a real kitchen," Gil says, lowering the gun.

"Why did you kill those people?" I say.

Gil leans against the wall. "They were bored."

I have no reply. I'm frightened that I understand Gil's logic, how merely existing counts for nothing. Gil walks to the door and opens it. "Stay there," he orders. The doorway swallows his image until it is simply an empty black rectangle. The darkness could be the edge of a flat world, I think. I could step outside and fall into the universe. Gil returns with his cookbook. He's left his shoulder bag in the car. "Take a look at this," he says. He tosses the book on my lap.

"What do you want me to look at?"

"The drawings."

The pages are stiff and yellowed. They smell like flour and soured oil. The text is broken up by simple illustrations, basic line-drawings of food and kitchen utensils. They are items a stick person might hold in a child's picture, nothing special. "What about them?" I ask.

"Read who did those. Read it out loud." Gil looks excited, pleased.

"'Drawings by Andrew Warhol,'" I read.

"Do you get it, brother?" Gil is nearly frantic. "*Andrew* Warhol. *Andrews* are geeks. You make fun of *Andrews*. They draw stupid pictures in cookbooks. They work night shifts at grocery stores. They get married because they're next in line."

I'm thinking to myself if I make it out alive: I hope this will all make sense. I hope I will understand how I came to be in a marginal motel situated on a back road in Riverside County. I will remember the smell of the lake and the moth slamming the sides of the lamp shade. All of this will be clear. But right now I am charged, as if every moment is a crackling static shock, thousands of blue-white sparks snapping all around me.

"You can change your circumstances," Gil says. "You're worthless if you don't. Look at me. I'm a headline. By tomorrow night I'm in the news. I'll *be* the news."

I start to speak but nothing comes out at first. The air is dry. I try again. "Those twelve people didn't ask for your help."

"They were practically dead anyway." Gil walks to the curtained window and parts it with his gun. "Besides, I'm almost done. Thirteen states is good. I wanted a dramatic number. But none of that jail shit for me. I couldn't take it. We're doing each other a favor, brother." Gil looks hard at me. "I'm crazy or evil. Is that what you are thinking?"

"Something like that." For a second, I consider rushing Gil.

"I'm no worse than a bad storm," Gil says. *"Thirteen Die in Flood. Tornado Kills Thirteen.* It's all the same." He's quiet for a few minutes, looking through the curtains and then back at me. "Our lives are going to change," he says softly, as if talking to himself, as if making plans. "Tomorrow there will be police and microphones and cameras. Nothing will be the same. The world will be listening. What are you going to say? How are you going to change your life?"

Gil lets the curtains close as he leans into the corner of the room. The night is still. There is no longer a moth, no voices. He looks at me and raises his weapon, pausing when it's pointed directly at me. Gil continues, holding the gun to the center of his own head, and shoots. The room shakes with the gunshot, Gil popping against the wall, falling forward.

I cannot move. I see Gil's hand and the blood running along his arm, turning maroon on the yellow carpet. I look at the door, waiting for someone to come, someone who heard the gunshot. The wall is a spray of blood and broken plaster. It looks like a garish painting, a red hibiscus with a white center. No one comes. Finally, I stand up. I don't look at Gil's body as I open the door. There are still no lights. It occurs to me to simply get in my car and leave. I could go home and pretend I was never here, hire a band, go to work. This does not seem feasible.

Except for this last part, that's the story. I stepped back inside. Gil's ponytail rested forward over much of the dark red exit wound. What do you do with a lifeless thing? What is the protocol? Gil was sprawled on the floor, a bad storm, an aberrant season in its own aftermath. I picked up his cookbook and walked outside, throwing it on the seat of my car next to the shoulder bag. The doorway of the motel room was a bright portal, a yellow of clarity.

I stood in front of that doorway knowing what was coming, what this was. I asked myself, what was my story? I was thinking about microphones and television, about police and *Andrews* transformed into *Andys*, about the chances handed to us, and those we manufacture on our own. What is the quota? How many can you afford to pass up? If the world comes to your door tonight and asks what happened, if anyone asks you any question, what can you say that will justify your life?

World Famous Love Acts

—||||||||—

F orgive my clairvoyance, sporadic and faulty as it is. I know we'll move on to other relationships after this, though none of them nearly as long or happy. "Goddamned flowers," you say as we pull away from your mother's house. "Tulips in spring. black-eyed Susans in summer. Mums in fall." And I feel bad because we see her just once a year and you always end up fighting. We're only here in the summer, and it's certain there'll be an argument. The first one was about the fact she liked to put hard candy in with the brewing coffee, her own flavoring technique. The mint really wasn't bad at all. And then, two years ago, that silly thing over your father's clothes. Why not let her keep them in the attic? And this time, she still hasn't sold his car. You're upset that it's sitting at the corner of the soybean field facing the interstate, black and dull as a dead beetle, surrounded by window-tall weeds. "Nobody wants that old thing," she keeps saying. And I know what you're thinking: how could she ask just nineteen hundred dollars?

"You're too upset," I say as I wave back at your mother. "Sometimes I don't know you."

"Just be sure of yourself," you say, "and you'll know me."

This is our last road trip and we both know it, two men, one pair of jeans each, three T-shirts, and gym cards for showers. After this, it's all over, though neither of us is saying anything and it's not because the old Toyota is worn out, dented and oxidized from too much Los Angeles sun. These summer visits to Indiana are more a vacation for our car than us, the thunderstorms, the shade of maple trees instead of wispy shadows of palm fronds. We can afford another car but this is it. I can't be sure right now of why, nor even of our impulse to hit the road like this. Except that we've heard about a place in New Orleans where people have sex on stage and both of us have to see that. "Maybe they'll ask for volunteers from the audience," you say as we pull farther away from your mother's white farmhouse, the dust behind us caught in the sun like rolling flame as we shoot down the dirt road. "I think New Orleans is going to be very important for us."

I look at you with a question.

"Road trip." You shrug. "Like old times." And what you mean is that you're never happier than when there's a long stretch of asphalt and white lines ahead of you. For you, the point is not to see. The point is to go.

"I can't wait," I say, but you make it sound as if this is some sort of reunion. I understand what happens after reunions.

You have the road atlas open on your lap and I see the blue line stretching through Atlanta, down to Savannah, down to Orlando (can't we skip the Magic Kingdom?) and back across to Louisiana where nightly, we hear, people have sex in front of an audience while waitresses keep the drinks full and strong. But that's in a few days and right now we're making the L-turn and your mom's house is way off on the right. Way off. Small as a doll's house. The first place we ever had sex. That initial summer, the whim of me joining you on the road. Pasadena to Muncie straight through. And your mother putting me on the couch downstairs on the fold-out, away from you upstairs in your old room. Her not-so-subtle hint about how badly the wood floors in the hall creak, how your dad just had to do something about them. The parental blockade was enough all by itself. Like a pro, you scooted along the bannister, avoided the floor, and slid down to me. Our mutual embarrassment that this was our first time, and both of us in our mid-twenties and still saying we were bi. Even then you liked adventure. Think of the zucchini you brought from the kitchen. Then the missionary position. We used that one for a long time, but how long has it been since we did even that? Maybe on this trip.

I know it's on your mind too, though you pretend to be captivated by the house you are always so anxious to leave. "She's getting old," you say.

"Not really," I say, but you don't even notice I'm contradicting you. You just keep looking out the window. We turn onto the interstate.

"There it is." Your hand points out the window, teeters in the wind.

"We could buy it ourselves."

"I wouldn't give her the satisfaction." But I know you want it, the car. I know you're thinking about all the Sunday trips with you in the back seat and your dad and mom up front. How many times have you talked about your father sneezing the loudest sneeze you've ever heard and swerving into a cornfield, too proud to stop and back up? Your mother laughing as your dad made a wide U-turn, thunk-thunking through the stalks, the only version of a jungle you could conceive of back then.

We're passing it, the car, and maybe it isn't black as a beetle. I'm thinking instead of a dirty jellybean, licorice flavored, a dull white *1,900* painted across its front window. Do you remember our first time in a car? That trip out to Barstow for your field tests. All those other seismologists, lesbians no less, and one of them having to share our room. But what a revelation. Okay, it was still the missionary position, but it was in a car. That, and the desert, that grayish blue of the evening, the cool we couldn't imagine would come after a day of one-hundred-plus. Nothing oral then, but we were good in that tiny space, both car doors open, room for our legs to hang outside. Afterward there was the swimming pool, a shard of blue in the darkness behind the motel. With us trying to be still in the center, bats flying by either side of us, skittering across the surface of the water as they drank. How could we go from that to being on the brink in nine years? I imagine the increments, the infatuation that wouldn't go away, the too-much sex that was still not enough for either of us, the driving around to estate sales on weekends while I started my furniture business, you in the passenger seat of that old van, helping me out, your day's wages: lunch or dinner and a quickie on one of the boulevards, in the parking lot of that lighting store, in the car wash. I think of those early forms of us and then now, and I wonder if this is how all couples end up?

We were close then. That's more important than you think. My sister told me about a man who called her in Des Moines. He explained that he was forty-seven. He had published thirty-three magazine articles and fourteen short stories which, added together, told exactly how old he was. He had also published seventy-four poems, the odd coincidence of being the mirror of his age. I'm sure my sister wasn't making this up. But this man said he was just plunking random numbers, and if it rang, he explained his situation like he did to my sister. At the end he said to her, "So, have you heard of me?"

Indianapolis isn't far off, a jagged lump on the bright horizon. That's the problem here, I think; the horizon. There are no landmarks. No hills to the east, ocean to the west. Nothing distinct. There's just this Midwest sun throwing down light like a wide-cast net. It's a shame the factory outlet on our left orients me, a row of brand-new empty business fronts.

"Would you want to touch anything that looked like that?" you ask, pointing at a radio station billboard. *20 Big Ones in a Row!* it says above illustrations of the upper half of ten super-busted blonde women in striped bikinis.

"Those look like something you toss around the stands at a baseball game," I say.

"I'm going to count," you say. "I'm going to see if those bastards play twenty songs in an hour. And if they're one tit short, I'll complain." You turn on the radio, looking for the right station, passing up twang after twang until you think you've got it right.

"That's a Cole Porter," I say. It's the Patty Lupone version of "Anything Goes."

"That can't be right. I don't see Cole Porter being endorsed by ten big-breasted women."

You shush me when I land on another station. "This is it." You take out a pen and make a mark on the corner of the road atlas. You really are going to count.

I guess we missed something because the disc jockey comes on after the song, laughing. So we spend the next hour listening to Van Halen, veering down and away from Indianapolis, Whitesnake, further, Aerosmith, further but you're keeping track even when our terrible radio starts to fuzz as we close in at the end of an hour. "Nineteen," you say. Metallica. "Twenty. They did it. Guess all those breasts didn't go to waste."

You turn off the radio and we're quiet for a short while. "What's this," you ask, holding up a small green brochure.

"Your mother gave it to me as an alternative to Sodom and Gomorrah."

You read. "Step inside Menno-Hof and begin your journey where the Mennonites and Amish began theirs: a sixteenth-century European courtyard. Learn how a simple pitcher of water transformed a peace-loving people into the most hunted outlaws in all Europe."

"Where is it, anyway?" I ask.

"In Shipshewana. That's north." You fold up the brochure and toss it into the back seat.

"Anything down here to see?"

"I understand all the limestone for the Empire State Building came from Indiana. There's probably a big hole to look at." I know you aren't a tourist. That's it for you.

I like your new summer haircut. Or maybe I just like the idea that you did it without even asking me. I didn't even question the idea of going to New Orleans to watch people having sex on stage. Though, as much as I've progressed, I've never told you about Tijuana and the donkey show I've heard of. Now that I think of it, it was you who first wanted to try something beyond missionary. I have to give you credit. Back then I couldn't conceive of anything else.

It was the one-year anniversary of your job at Cal Tech. Twelve months of employment. Your apartment had gone art deco, half-oval sconces, the armoire I gave you for the new television and stereo, all that angular wood inlay, the picture frames changed. You even replaced the bleached-pine trim around the ceilings. Your bedroom all silver and gray. In the dim Los Angeles mornings we could almost believe we were living in black and white.

So that morning you woke up, twelve paychecks under your belt, a year to the day. You had money. We had money and we were happy. We started to make love on your bed the usual way but you stopped. "I want to try something new," you said. You took me outside to the patio, both of us naked and in full view of any other early morning tenants. The air was heavy with the dusty smell of hibiscus, and the sun was little more than a vague pink theory beyond the foothills.

"What if we get caught?" I said, but you put your finger to my lips, and I remember that it smelled like maple syrup.

"We'll only get caught if you keep talking," you whispered. So we stood there, kissing, made love standing up, and your skin was warm on me in a different way, not the warmth of forced pressure, but something softer, the gaps between our bodies opening and closing allowing cool air to sift between us.

If you ever ask me how much I love you, I'd answer with this detail: when we stood on the patio making love, my feet never moved. I remember, because at one point I felt something wet and I looked down and saw a large snail tracing across the top of my foot. I endured its slow, unpleasant streak, let it be part of our moment so it wouldn't have to disrupt your fantasy. I was proud all morning of that silvery trail across my foot. It all seems so innocent now. We were just standing up, but we were equalized and that seemed right.

"I like a good snout," you say just outside Atlanta. No sex at the rest stop last night. Just a little sleep. We've been quiet since we woke and you're driving. "Yes," you say, "I like good snout. A healthy proboscis."

I'm not sure what brought this on, though I suspect the bloodhound in the back of a rust-pocked pickup truck in front of us. "On people?" I ask.

"Of course. I used to go in for small noses, but my tastes have definitely shifted."

I put my hand to my own nose. "And where does mine fit in?"

"I wasn't talking about you," you say, giving me a light punch in the shoulder.

I'm still feeling my nose. "But let's just say you are. What about it?"

You give me a good, hard look and then turn back to the road. Outside, the sumac is giving way to tall, straggly pines. It's a dry summer and the periphery is a whir of yellow-green. "You don't have anything to worry about, Bit," you say. "Your nose is adequate."

Adequate. How do you get around a word like that? Especially after my old nickname. I never came up with one for you. You switch lanes and we pull up alongside of the dog and the pickup. It holds its head over the side, facing directly into the wind, ears and jowls flapping like brown socks on a clothesline. Its large black nose shines and flares slightly. I've heard that dogs like this can detect a particular scent in the tiniest fractions and I wonder if this dog is up there because the world is going through his nose at seventy miles an hour and he's just getting high.

"Would you consider rhinoplasty if I asked you?" you say.

"Would you ask me?"

"I suppose not."

I'm not surprised that this even comes up. We're both pretty vain. It's probably the reason we decided against the baby, if you could call it a decision. Both of us inexplicably depressed for months, having sex to fix it, doing it from the side too, by then, sharing top and bottom, and still we were depressed and then the baby idea, something to rally around. But it wasn't the adopting that brought us together. It was the decision not to.

I remember exactly. You lived on Mulholland Way, not Drive, we told people. Not where movie stars' homes overlook Los Angeles. We were below, where your address, 1940 Mulholland Way, had its own fame. You were right on the corner in that Spanish-style duplex that was all about curves, from the thick stucco to the arched windows and oak door. But the biggest curve wasn't part of the house. It was just up the street; on Friday and Saturday nights we got used to the fact that someone would come around too fast and not see how the road straightened out and smash into the wall.

The night we decided about the baby, the little girl in China we knew we could get, we were having angel-hair pasta with the fresh marinara I made from scratch in your kitchen. "We shouldn't accept it," you said. "Selfish people shouldn't have kids."

"We could get married," I said. "Kind of." And you just stared at me. I didn't think very clearly then. I made that whole dinner because I thought it would make things easier, the crabmeat cocktail, baked onion soup, endive salad, the pasta, the from-scratch breadsticks, and burnt-sugar cake. I don't think you ever noticed how I set the table, a water and wineglass, two main forks and napkin to the left of the plate, knives and spoon to the right, with the seafood fork angled into the spoon. All of it was proper.

"We can't get married," you said, a bolt of pasta waiting at the end of your fork.

"Especially not for this reason. You just can't fake a family."

"It just seems logical."

"If you want to talk logical," you said, "get me some black pepper from the spouse rack."

I would have laughed, but instead I got you the pepper. Then you gave me the most direct look I've ever seen from you.

"You're the best person I know," you said. "I don't say that enough."

For once, I'd been the one who wanted it. And maybe you were right. What would we do now if we had a little Jella or Keena? It would be in school by now, bringing home paintings of lopsided houses and suns so close to the earth they'd seem like predictions of the apocalypse. So, no baby, but we did make a commitment to be alone together for a very long time.

We're almost into Atlanta, the city itself. The morning sky is a bluish yellow, creased with thin clouds like wax-paper wrinkles. It's already warm outside, slightly humid, and the air smells like bread; not cornbread—white bread. "Do you smell that?" I ask.

You keep one hand on the wheel and unroll the window. "Burning leaves?"

"Never mind," I say. "Should we stop anywhere?"

"Not unless Rhett and Scarlet are thumbing it on the side of the road."

I want to ask you if we can get out and walk around. I want to ask if we can just slow up a bit, if for once we wouldn't rush through. But I know what you're thinking: still morning, enough time to get to Savannah, press on. And so I flip my seat back. "Wake me when we get to Savannah," I say. But part of me wants to pick a fight to show how good a couple we are.

"Okay, Bit," you say and you wink. "I'll wake you if I see a good patch of kudzu."

I feel a poke in the side. "You want to see this?" you ask. "A bunch of Spanish moss and crap."

I sit up, roused at the tail end of a dream about our trip to Washington D.C. Outside we drive down a main road bordered by black-barked trees closing over us. The branches are necklaced with thick, dangling strands of grayish-green moss that slim to fine points. The houses on this stretch are broad-porched, each painted a variation of white or yellow. The windows are curtained by material so thin you can almost see through the diamond-latticed windows. I unroll my window for a better look, and the heat whooshes in along with an almost unreal dampness. I immediately roll the window back up.

"Remember the squirrels?" I ask.

You laugh. "In D.C.?"

"I was dreaming about them." That was one of our first real road trips. It took us an hour to find a parking spot once we got into the city, and by then, as usual, you were ready to leave. But at least you let us stop at the Jefferson Memorial with its curve of not-yet-in-bloom cherry trees, one of them with a hollow trunk and a dozen or so dead, gutted squirrels strewn about, each with three heads-up pennies placed on the inside spine. At the base of the tree were nineteen dollar bills laid out end to end and a line of sixty pennies. Neither of us were even tempted to take the money. "That was our first dangerous sex," I say.

You think for a moment before saying anything. "Was that before the TransAmerica building?"

"Yes," I say. That was a later road trip, a quickie to San Francisco and the unavoidable sex in the foggy night, up against the bracing of that building you called a "phallic wonder." We had a bottle of lube, so San Francisco had to be after. "D.C. was a year earlier," I say. "I'm sure of it."

"All I remember," you say, "is that you wouldn't go down on me in front of Jefferson."

"But all we had to do was step behind the statue and I was fine." Both of us laugh but I know your laughing because these memories confirm your notions that I'm not as experimental, that I'm more Puritan compared to you. Outside, the mossy canopy opens like the light end of a tunnel, and the bright sun flattens out the landscape. The refraction off glass and metal is startling, as if this newer part of Savannah is just moments away from combustion.

"Why don't we do anything like that anymore?" I say.

"We could," you offer, but there's no conviction behind it.

"Tonight?" I shuffle my feet a bit, sifting through candy wrappers and potato chip bags.

"Let's not plan it," you say. "It has to be spontaneous." And then, quick as a sniper on a tower, you change the subject. It's the kind of abruptness I can never get away with. "I thought we'd drive out to the Atlantic. We've never been."

We pass a sign that reads *Tybee Island*. I unroll the window for the smell of salt because I can tell we're getting close to the ocean. On either side of us are great stretches of tall grass ribboned with wide blue water where small boats leave temporary white scratches on the surface.

"Are you having a moment?" you ask and I know exactly what you're talking about, one of my clairvoyant spells.

"No," I say. "I'm just watching the boats. I haven't had a full-blown moment since Wallace." You mocked me a bit about that, just a bit. Wallace was giving me a ride in his new car when we got pulled over by LAPD. The whole time he and the cop were very polite to one another but I sensed something more. The cop was thinking *Must be something up if this black guy is driving a brand-new car.* And every time Wallace said "Yes, Officer," he was thinking *Son of a bitch. I know what's up.* After Wallace signed the citation and we started back on the road I said, "It really sucks the way he treated you."

Wallace looked at me and said, "What way?"

"Hassling a black man with a new car."

Wallace gave me a hard, corrective look. "I was going twenty miles over the speed limit," he said.

Later that night, when I told you all this, you laughed. "You mean well," you said, patting my head like I was a child. "You've just got a little Sputnik inside you sending mysterious transmissions."

The oceanfront is obscured by rows of houses and summer rental units, but you find us a parking spot right next to a stairway to the beach. The air is surprisingly calm and though I can see the grass-freckled dunes, it seems too quiet to be close to the water. We walk along a wooden path to the peak of the dunes where a green-and-white sign tells us not to pick the sea oats—

tall, thin grass that looks like hairs on a balding scalp. I tap you on the shoulder to see if you see what I see in the cleavage of a pair of small dunes: two men having sex.

You shake your head and pull me onward. "You'll have plenty of time for voyeurism in New Orleans."

At the end of the walk, the Atlantic spreads out before us. The bright, open sky and dark water come together like bolts of stacked linen. Suddenly you're taking off your sandals and running toward the water. I follow.

The water is surprisingly cool and timid around our ankles. The waves here are not like the Pacific. They seem tentative, weak pulses straggling toward shore. And not another person on the beach as far as I can see in both directions. Summer and this broad stretch of white sand with its band of darkness nearest the water, and no one enjoying it but us. I look up to the dunes but I can't see the two men, just a long line of beach fencing, wavy as the picked-clean bones of an eel.

You bury your feet just where the wave is deepest, where it feels like a last breath before retreating. "We've never stood right here," you say. You close your eyes and smile and I know not to say anything. New ground is important to you.

We've never been here before, it's true. We've never been to the Atlantic at all. Would I have ever been to London or Paris without you? Or New York and the closed-off subway terminal below the World Trade Center where you pushed me up against the wall and told me what to do? I learned to take orders then, listened carefully for where to put my hands, where to put my mouth. You taught me.

So I watch you now, jeans rolled up to your knees, speckled with water, white T-shirt glaring in the sun and still not as fine as your smile, the one I see so little now, and I know I still love you and I don't want to be done learning. I don't want this to be our last trip together, though I'm almost sure it is. I think we're seeing the end.

Florida is on fire. We saw it long before they diverted us away from continuing south, the hazy, brown smoke looking like a miles-wide waterfall defying gravity, flowing upward, the high altitude winds scraping the top flat, making a river of smoke flow west. But I keep driving, unconcerned. In Los Angeles, these colors and wildfires mean it's fall. It's a ritual. The Santa Ana winds rush in like hungry gods, stroking the hillsides until they find someone with a match and a problem. And then we sacrifice, the whole city gathers around televisions to see how many homes will go up. And what's left behind are the sunsets, smoke-induced variations on amber. Browns and yellows you can't call brown and yellow, maybe cocoa, maybe the gold of Spanish coins. "L.A.'s version of a rainbow," you once said.

They've diverted us west and the fire flanks us almost at the edge of the freeway. The smoke here is black, melting out of huge orange columns. An early red-white-and-blue campaign billboard stands just above the flames. There's a large photo of a jowly, pearly-haired man with unruly brows that dip over his eyes. *Rutch Hodgins Independent for U.S. Senator.* Someone has spray painted over the "e" so that it reads Sinator.

"I read about that guy," you say. "He got married last year. She was nineteen and he was eighty." Then you growl and put your seat back and I know you are frustrated that there's so much traffic ahead of us, that we can't just go and be done with the fire. "When I was a child," you say, "my grandparents' house caught on fire a week before Christmas. They lost everything. And this is the part I never understand." You sit back up and look at me. "My grandparents came to stay with us and my parents took down the Christmas tree and put all the presents in the church donation box. All my dad said was, 'No Christmas this year.'"

"Wow," I say, "you never told me that story before."

"Really? I thought we'd said everything to each other we could possibly say."

"Is that a good or bad thing?" I ask, just as we get beyond the fire line. Ahead I see the detour for southbound traffic, which is us.

"I guess it depends on if you like to talk. I'm fine with it."

But I'm not fine with it. "Shouldn't we always have something to say?"

You pause for a moment. "Silence between two people can say a great deal," you offer.

I take your cue. I have this feeling we've climbed down a length of very long rope only to come to an impossibly frayed end. And you're content to just hang here, maybe even let go.

The detour takes us off the highway and over a series of increasingly narrow roads. The land on either side is parched, yellow and flat, not a single green lawn in front of the few houses here and there, all of them squat like half-melted candles. We're following a trailer-pulled car, a dusty-red wagon with orange-centered taillights like jet engines and chrome-trimmed tail fins jutting out like horn-rimmed glasses.

"The back of that car reminds me of my mother," you say, "when she used to wear those awful black bifocals."

"There," I yell. "I was just thinking that. The thing about the glasses."

You don't even have to ask. I can see you understand I'm talking about my clairvoyance. You just shake your head. I look out the window. There are more houses here. We're getting closer to a town. "There's a kid home from school with lice," I say. "His parents have shaved his head and he's been watching soap operas all day. The doorbell rings. It's a woman, a neighbor. She's surprised. 'I've got lice,' the boy says.

"'Tell your Dad I'll come back later,' she says. 'Will you be here tomorrow?' The boy shakes his head and goes back to the TV. His dad comes in the room. 'That was Mrs. Ebersol,' the boy says. The father is a bit flustered. 'Dad?' the boy asks. 'Do we use tampons?' '*We* don't,' the father laughs, 'but your mother does.' The boy nods and turns toward the television. 'If we go to the store,' he says over his shoulder, I can show you which ones are the most absorbent.'"

"Come on," you finally break in. "You're making that up."

"No." I want to be more adamant, wave my hands or something, but I'm driving.

"You are not psychic."

"Clairvoyant," I say. "How do you explain what I see if I'm not?"

"Your imagination is a flower with an invisible stem," you say.

"I can tell the difference. This stuff I see really happens."

You're silent for miles but finally you feel sorry for me. I want to tell you I know you feel sorry for me, but we'll just start all over again. Then you offer me a consolation. "What brand does the kid recommend?"

We roll into a slim strip of a town. Every restaurant parking lot is full. All this diverted traffic must be a boon. Both of us are hot and I pull into the Airy Queen, the capital "D" and lowercase "a" painted over, changed. There's something about Florida and signs and paint.

Inside, we sit across from each other over our drinks without letting the straws from our lips. Here too, every logo has been altered to say Airy Queen. They're not even trying to be subtle. I know you notice all this, too—the never-changed red seats and scratched, white tabletops, the teenage boy mopping the floor in a generic blue uniform, rolls of neck-fat curled over his collar. You look around and approve of the minimal remodeling. "It's like a hundred-year-old woman buying a new coat," you say. "Why bother?"

"As long as the sodas are cold." My straw gurgles at the bottom of my already-empty cup and I look up at you. I want to know. "What's happening?" I ask.

"We've been together a long time. I guess this is the part where we learn to enjoy not having to surprise each other."

Before I can say anything, the kid mopping the floor arrives near our table and swipes the blackish mop near our feet, squeezing it into a bucket of even blacker water. "This is about the busiest day we've had since I've been here," he says. We nod, thinking he's going to continue mopping, but he leans for a moment on his mop handle. "Where you two from?" He's thick, pimply, and has a wheezy voice. He wears a gold name tag with no imprint.

"Los Angeles," I say. "Pasadena."

The kid considers this for a moment and smiles. "You all are going to have an earthquake that cracks California right off into the ocean." I know you won't let that pass. I remember once you had an argument with a woman at the bookstore. You insisted that H.G. Wells was scientifically unsound.

"Actually," you tell the kid with the mop, giving me a small kick under the table, "it's the other way around. I'm a seismologist." The kid looks confused, so you say, "We're the people who figure out how strong an earthquake is."

"Seismologist," the kid repeats as if he understands.

"When the big one hits," you continue, "it isn't California that's going to fall into the ocean. We figured out the rest of the continent is kind of supported by the West Coast, like a bearing wall. We figure everything past the Sierra Nevadas is going to sink into the Atlantic."

"Really?" the kid asks, but he's looking at me.

"I just sell antique furniture," I say.

He looks at you. "Really?"

"It's fifty-fifty," you say. "Why do you think so many people move to California?"

The kid shakes his head and starts mopping again. He's probably thinking about how much money he has to save to move. You're trying not to laugh and you have that look on your face, the proud one, high eyebrows, pinched smile. It's the same look you had the night we watched the wildfire sunset that you said was like a rainbow. We were on the roof of a parking garage in Pasadena after an early dinner. It was the top floor and we had the only car on that level. You walked me to the corner with this same smile, and we watched the sun go down. We were behind a large exhaust vent and started kissing, all of Old Town spread out below us. "I want to try something," you whispered in my ear. You undid my clothes, stripped me, and turned me toward the city, the yellow streetlights popping on just at the moment, etching new color on the brick buildings. Then you put two of your fingers in my mouth and moved them around slowly. You took them out and suddenly you were doing something new, using them in me, first one, then both, gently sliding in and out, touching a spot inside that felt like small electric shocks each time you made a pass, until in one surprising moment I came. You kissed me on the back of the neck and I braced myself on the ledge with both hands, my legs quivering slightly. "I'll meet you in the car," you said.

The sun is getting low, looking hollow and smoke-orange. It cuts a molten swath between the buildings, over the long line of diverted traffic and into the big glass window that separates us from the outside. On the table next to us is a newspaper. One of the headlines says *Aids Wanted*. I look at it long enough to understand it's an article about assisting the elderly. I pick up my cup and pat some ice into my mouth. You don't seem to be thinking anything. If anyone had asked, I'd never have told them that this is how we'd end up, satisfied by silence in a failed ice-cream franchise. You stand up, ready to go, but I don't move. "I want to know what's wrong with us. Why aren't we in love anymore?"

Now you look impatient, running your straw in and out of the lid of your cup. This is how you always get if I persist, if I insist on any kind of definition. "Sex does not equal love," you say. "I care for you without having sex." And then you lean in on the table, run a hand through your hair, and look at me hard. "We've had so much sex, we've run up a surplus. It's not going to be like it was."

"Never?"

"Not soon. That part of us is over, at least the amount." You smile and put your hand on mine, which is unusual for you. No public displays of gentle affection. "We just have different ideas about love. I'm starting to think it's as simple as a debt between two people."

Your hand touching mine is surprisingly cold, probably from your cup. You pull it away.

"What do you think we owe each other?" I ask.

"I'd never have gotten the Cal Tech gig without you," you say. "You pushed me. And maybe I've dragged your flat ass out of a life of predictability. And you've got employees now."

I smile. You smile. "On behalf of the flat-ass clan, I thank you," I say.

"So *that's* love," you say, and like a tractor plowing through a pile of loose hay, you add, "and sometimes love isn't a good enough excuse to stay together."

It's early evening and we're on the road north. Skipping the Magic Kingdom. Did I predict that or just wish it? I didn't ask what you

meant back there in Airy Queen because I was afraid. I just gave a
noncommittal nod hoping that would pass. The sky to the west is
a thin bluish-beige line. No Orlando means no gym and no shower
for each of us. We'll be ripe for New Orleans. Since you want to
drive the last stretch, I slide down in my seat and close my eyes,
thinking about the people on stage getting paid for having sex, the
people I know we'll see. I think of black men with wide shoulders
and tight skin slimming down to abs like unseeded garden rows,
tight, muscled hips and all of it a slick arrow coming to a point in
a big dark penis, and white guys with pink nipples and that kind
of creaminess their skin takes on with sex sweat, the dark pubic
hair over dicks that never get so long but plump up if girth is your
thing, and white women, slender as boned fish but somehow
keeping all the curves, asses smooth as sand dunes and silent
blonde hair that wants to fall over their eyes, black women bigger
dunes, a wideness that asserts itself, skin that darkens just right at
the joints, and breasts that aren't for amateurs. I think of all of
them, the men and women with their sweet spots and those places
where fingers and tongues belong. This is what we'll see in New
Orleans. This is what's going to remind you how it was for us.

We've stopped. I open my eyes slightly and you're lying back in
your seat, eyes staring at the ceiling of the car. It's hot, so hot my
back is completely wet. I guess you got tired. I reach over and
touch your hand and you look at me. "Can we try?" I ask.

"Sure," you say.

I roll over to kiss you. We're in the dim corner of a rest stop.
"Where are we?"

"Somewhere."

I look into your eyes. I look. I do not remember how to kiss you. I tell you this.

"That's okay," you say and you undo your belt and mine. We take off our wet T-shirts and slide our pants to our ankles. These bodies should know each other. I reach for my gym bag but you stop me. "No toys. Let's just use our hands," you say. "We don't want to get too messy."

I'm above you, naked, not wanting to touch you because of the heat, constricted by the space and the pants around my ankles, the steering wheel in my back, not even remembering how to touch you, afraid to do the wrong thing. We start to laugh on some mutual cue and the moment is over.

"What now?" I ask.

"Let's put on our clothes and finish the trip," you say.

I've been standing in front of the same New Orleans crypt for half an hour trying to figure this out. The liquid brown thickness at the bottom of the candle jar is a soup of dead cockroaches. They are fermenting in layers, progressively lightening until the top with its five struggling roaches trying to escape the glass. The jar sits in front of this wall of granite. Above the name is the carved, weathered image of a robed woman, sitting, her hand to her forehead in grief, a cracked planter of water-starved purple vines stretching upward against the stone. Next to it is the cockroach jar, and just above, one readable date, *1899*.

The cockroaches skitter on their hind legs, standing against the glass walls of the jar. I wonder if this is part of a curse or a prayer, a long grudge or unsuppressed hope. It is late afternoon, so hot and humid I'm sweating from just standing. Long shadows shift in intensity as empty thunderclouds pass over the sun. I see you at the front of the cemetery. The car fits perfectly in the entrance space. The walls begin on either side of you, all crypts as well, crumbling red brick between each arched coffin space, stacked three high all the way around. The center is filled with thick rows of gray-stone crypts, some of them with fifteen sealed coffins. Nearly all of them are surrounded by wrought iron and crowned by eroded crosses or decapitated saints. Many facades have crumbled, revealing simple brick and mortar. And there you are in our gray Toyota, the gatekeeper. You honk. It's time to go.

On the outer wall of the cemetery is a flyer with hand-cut phone number strips. It says *Earn $2,000 a week from your home*. I tear off a number. "Here," I say as I get back in the car, into the shock of air-conditioning. "Quit your job and let's move. Two thousand a week for just sitting at home."

"Thanks," you say, "but I'm still waiting for the right pyramid scheme. Did you get enough?"

You're talking about my insistence that we stop at a cemetery. I want to tell you about the cockroaches, how I want to go back and save them, how I was afraid of some voodoo backlash, a sudden spinal pain, but I just nod and you start the car. When I was a child in Blue Falls, after the first heavy, cold rains that rolled over the Columbia, I'd go out into the street and save earthworms from the puddles, toss them onto lawns or flower beds and give them a second chance. Now I wonder if I was messing with something bigger than I thought. If I screwed up some master plan and I'm paying for it now.

"We can head for the French Quarter," you say, "find a parking space, and look for the place."

"I wish we knew the name."

"We'll find it."

You drive on instinct and it doesn't take us long before we're stuck behind a mule-driven cart with two thick-browed tourists riding in the back. The driver wears a trim straw hat with a black band, the whip in his gravy-brown hands, a slender pole hanging at a not so threatening angle to the right.

It feels as if we're driving through slightly enlarged versions of the crypts, close-packed buildings, wrought iron, French windows instead of coffin spaces. But maybe the difference is that everything here is held together somehow by a tenuous coat of newness. The white trim is sharp in the late afternoon light, and the ironwork of the sagging balconies looks sturdy somehow, thickened by years of paint. I feel suddenly optimistic, as if everything between us is going to be all right.

"Look for the place," you tell me.

"What are we looking for?"

You give me a tight look of frustration. "I'm not sure. Something that says *Sex Show,* I suppose." You make a turn so we're not behind the mule cart anymore but it puts us behind another, this one black as a hearse, a family in the back and the driver pointing at every other building. We drive like this for fifteen minutes until you will a space on the street and a car pulls out from the curb and we slip in.

We walk to Bourbon Street, past a shop with stacked, glazed heads of baby alligators, jaws in midsnap, past a screened club-window with the silhouette of a woman dancing topless, past a completely silver-coated woman wearing a silver toga and holding silver grapes, standing still as a statue for contributions in her silver dish. What makes us stop is a man in a tight black turtleneck. He stands at the door of a bar. "You two sweethearts look hot," he says in a quiet lisp. His toupee is too thick and too dark for his age. He's wearing makeup, foundation. "Free Jell-O shooters for the next hour." We walk on.

Even in the fading daylight it's not getting any cooler. My hair sticks to my forehead. The air is like a drop cloth of invisible steam. It smells like wet concrete and alcohol and urine. It smells sweet. And except for washing down in a rest-stop bathroom, neither of us have bathed in two days.

"We should've brought shorts," you say, tapping me on the leg to indicate you're stopping for a beer. The bar stands open to the street, blue neon light spilling onto the sidewalk like pooled water. Just beyond that, a group of black kids, boys, smash aluminum cans, and attach them to their worn tennis sneakers. One of them is already done. His red cap sits in front of him, already seeded with some change and a dollar bill. He scrapes out a beat, a scratchy tap dance. Sometimes I feel like I'm doing this same thing for you.

You come out with two beers. Across the street, trombone-heavy Dixieland breaks out and on our side, an electric guitar starts the blues. This seems to be the call. The sidewalks begin to fill with more people. Things are suddenly in gear, and now that I've something to compare myself to, I realize I'm tired.

You tug at my elbow and point. A large sign bordered by flashing light bulbs says *World Famous Love Acts*. "Do you think that's it?"

"Maybe," I say. We walk over to take a closer look. This is the place. The outside walls are covered with faded photographs of discretely posed men and women in sexual positions, nothing we haven't tried. They are on a small stage, the men wearing tight gold lamé bikini shorts, the women the same, with string tops. None of them are in shape and they're smiling, not out of pleasure, but almost like they're winning at a game. One couple is posed in the doggie position. The man's hairy gut rests on the woman's ass as she stares at the camera, bleached blonde hair falling in front of her half-lidded eyes. Above all this is a smaller sign that reads *World Famous Love Acts. The most erotic spot on earth! Come in and take home what you learn! You'll never be the same!*

"Not as impressive when you see it all in front of you like that," you say, a tilt to your head as you examine the photographs. You sound matter-of-fact, like this is something you expected all along.

"Maybe it's better inside," I say.

You look at me and speak softly. "Be honest, Bit. Would they have *these* pictures on the *outside* if it was any better on the inside?"

A woman in shiny copper-colored sarong steps out of the doorway with a stack of slim papers in hand, a blare of slow rock following her before it's pinched off by the closing door. "You two oughta come in," she says, winking, allowing us a full view of her bright green eye shadow. She holds out two of the papers. "A drink on the house."

"Do they have their clothes on the whole time?" you ask her.

The woman smiles. Her red lipstick shines under the flashing lights. "We can't talk about the love acts on the street. But I promise you'll have a wild time." She continues holding out the drink tickets.

You grab my hand and turn to me, eyes wide open, eyebrows high. "What do you think?"

"To be honest," I say, "I'm tired." But what I want to say is that I can't believe you're holding my hand again. I want to say I already know what you're thinking. That you love me. That we don't need this. We should just go off and be by ourselves. That all along we both knew that this wasn't going to be the climax of our road trip. You understand the same thing I do, that we're in this for the long haul and this show won't mean anything to us. We know how to have sex and we're going to. It's not over. If I've ever had a truly clairvoyant moment, it's now. I can see what you're thinking. I can see the future. "I feel like we've been on the road a hundred years," I say.

"You're reading my mind," you answer, and you give me an odd look of sympathy. You turn to the woman, letting go of my hand, emptying the space between us. "I'm sorry," you tell her. "It's been a long century and we're exhausted."

THE AUTHOR

Born to a Chinese father and Euro-American mother, **Brian Leung** is a native of San Diego, California. He received an MFA in Creative Writing from Indiana University. His fiction and poetry have appeared in *Story, Crazyhorse, Grain, Gulf Coast, Kinesis, Mid-American Review, Salt Hill, Gulf Stream, River City, The Bellingham Review,* and *The Connecticut Review.* He lives in Los Angeles, where he is an Assistant Professor at California State University, Northridge.